AN ENCHANTED KNIGHT

THE CURSED KINGDOM

HILDIE McQUEEN

USA TODAY BESTSELLING AUTHOR

OLIVERHEBERBOOKS

All rights reserved.

No part of this publication may be sold, copied, distributed, reproduced or transmitted in any form or by any means, mechanical or digital, including photocopying and recording or by any information storage and retrieval system without the prior written permission of both the publisher, Oliver Heber Books and the author, Hildie McQueen, except in the case of brief quotations embodied in critical articles and reviews.

PUBLISHER'S NOTE: This is a work of fiction. Names, characters, places, and incidents either are the product of the author's imagination or are used fictitiously. Any resemblance to actual persons, living or dead, business establishments, events, or locales is entirely coincidental.

An Enchanted Knight Copyright 2025 © Hildie McQueen

Cover art by Dar Albert, Wicked Smart Designs

Published by Oliver-Heber Books

0 9 8 7 6 5 4 3 2 1

Chapter One

DUNIMARLE CASTLE
CULROSS, SCOTLAND

The castle stood like a relic of Scotland's past, its ancient walls steeped in mystery and magic. From the moment Gwen Lockhart set foot on the grounds, she felt it—a pulse of something otherworldly woven into the very stones. As a seasoned medium, Gwen was no stranger to the supernatural, but this place was different. The air thrummed with the whispers of spirits long gone, their presence lingering in the shadows of the centuries-old halls.

This wasn't just another job—it was the kind of assignment that promised to be unforgettable.

Gwen froze at the entryway into the large sitting room. A man stood by the large front window as he had just the day before. His gaze intent on whatever he spied on the horizon.

The scenery outside, extraordinarily different from when he'd lived there, in the same castle.

Not just different.

Hundreds of years had passed.

The striking male seemed lost in thought.

The way he stood, posture erect, hand on the hilt of the sword at his hip, told of self-assurance. He was lord and master of any space he inhabited. His dark emerald-green belted tunic and tan breeches had to have been tailor-made because they fit his powerful physique perfectly.

By his manner of dress, he'd lived sometime in medieval times.

As far as he was concerned, it was still that time, long past.

To him, at least.

HER SHARP INTAKE of breath couldn't be stopped when he finally turned to look at her. His piercing green eyes conveyed a myriad of emotions when they locked to hers. Anger, frustration, dismay, and hope flickered in rapid succession.

Gwen's mouth fell open, but no sound came as she attempted to control her racing heartbeat. At the same time she froze, unwilling to move, not wishing for him to disappear.

The presence was solid, tangible, stronger than any she'd ever encountered.

Although his fingers tightened around the sword's hilt, he maintained a calm façade.

The telltale tightening of his jaw gave away an underlying tension. He reminded her of a river near her home, where the calmness of the water's surface lulled many an unsuspecting swimmer to their death, the turbulent undercurrents catching them unawares.

"Ye are my enchantress. Ye must free me."

It wasn't a spoken request, for his lips never moved, but Gwen heard the words loud and clear.

"Who are you?" She asked out loud. The question was a delay tactic, because she knew his identity and hoped to lure him to remain longer.

"Free me," he repeated more urgently.

"From what?"

The man shook his head, fading.

"Wait," Gwen called out as he vanished.

"You saw him, Tristan?" Edith McRainey, the current estate's owner, spoke behind her, causing Gwen to jump. The older lady gave her a quizzical look.

"You've just seen him again, haven't you?" she asked, not seeming a bit surprised.

Casually elegant in grey slacks and a lavender two-piece sweater set, salt-and-pepper hair swept up into an elegant chignon, Edith was eternally stylish.

The older woman's lips curved, her sparkling blue eyes meeting Gwen's. "I just knew it had to be you as soon as you walked through the door. I was convinced you were the one."

The woman walked into the room and looked around as if expecting to see the ghost as well. She let out a small disappointed sigh at not spying him.

"He's never reappeared so soon. It was just yesterday

morning you spotted him for the first time." With a bright smile, she waited for Gwen to speak.

Gwen couldn't help but smile back. Edith McRainey was a likable woman and her Scottish lilt enchanting.

"Ms. McRainey, I don't know if it was him or not, but there is definitely an entity in this house." She glanced toward the window where he'd stood and resisted the urge to move closer to the spot.

"If only you had the portrait, it would be helpful in confirming that the man I just saw is indeed your ancestor, Tristan McRainey."

"Oh dear." Edith's eyebrows pinched together. "I have no idea what happened to Tristan's portrait and why it's suddenly gone missing."

The slight woman shook her head, her face sagging. "Tomorrow when my nephew Derrick arrives, he is bringing a photo of a portrait and a miniature of Tristan that my brother, his father, kept. Perhaps Derrick can also shed some light on where the larger portrait is. Always fielding calls, he ended our conversation earlier on the phone, before I could ask him."

Edith slid past her to the hallway entrance and peered at a bare spot on the wall, a large anchor the only visible evidence that a portrait hung there.

"Tristan McRainey's portrait has always been in the same place, here in the hallway outside the sitting room, just as he instructed in his Last Will and Testament. Perhaps, it's been gone for a while, and because I've gotten so used to it being there, I didn't notice it was missing right away."

She pressed her hands into her chest and shook her head. "I've failed him."

Gwen approached the woman and patted her shoulder in an effort to reassure her. "I'm sure you'll find it. There has to be a good explanation for its disappearance."

They moved back into the sitting room, and Gwen couldn't help but look at the window again. Why had the apparition stood by the window both times? It had to be Tristan McRainey, the long-since deceased laird of the castle she now visited.

Edith must have ordered tea, because just then one of the home's staff members came in with a tray of tea and placed it down on the coffee table. The young girl smiled shyly at Gwen and waited to serve them. After they sat, she proceeded to pour for them and left.

"Thank you, Lizzie." Edith McRainey watched Gwen expectantly while sipping her tea.

Gwen took her journal and pen out of her tote bag and opened the book to a fresh page.

"Mrs. McRainey," she began.

"Please call me Edith. Since you accepted the assignment in the matter of Tristan McRainey, to help free him, you'll be here for some time, getting to know my family background quite well. We might as well be on a first-name basis."

"Okay then, Edith." Gwen smiled at the woman who didn't resemble the ghost in the least.

Gwen wasn't sure the male she'd seen earlier had smiled often while he'd lived. He seemed more the brooding type.

"Edith, can you describe Laird McRainey? What you

remember from the portraits, of course, since he died a long time before you were born."

Gwen wrote the date and time at the top of the page before adding, "It's helpful for me to know as much as possible about him. It's imperative that you give me as much information as you can, so that I can help him move on and finally be at peace."

"At peace?"

"Yes, I assume you hired me to do what I do best. Help Tristan McRainey move past where he has been. In limbo... perhaps not a good choice of words." Gwen searched for a better explanation, not quite sure why words eluded her. "I help people who've passed away find their path, move to the beyond, where they can find eternal rest."

"Oh no dear. You misunderstand. He's not dead," Edith replied, alarm tightening her face. She set her teacup down so hard the cup bounced in the small saucer.

Meeting Gwen's gaze, she gave her an expectant look. "I haven't hired you to expel a ghost. Quite the contrary—you're here to free the Laird McRainey. Release him from the enchantment."

"Release him? I don't understand."

Edith's clear eyes locked onto Gwen's. "You, dear girl, are his only hope for rejoining the living."

Chapter Two

A man trapped in an alternate world, imprisoned by a dark wizard, waiting for a woman to cast the spell that would free him—it sounded like something from a fairy tale. Yet, her hostess, Edith, insisted it was all true. More than that, Edith was certain Gwen's repeated encounters with Tristan McRainey meant one thing: she was "the one" destined to break the curse.

As Edith recounted the story—what little she knew—Gwen scribbled notes furiously, her mind spinning with disbelief and curiosity. Could any of this be real?

Later, Gwen retreated to the second floor, her thoughts still tangled in the bizarre tale. The bedroom was a serene contrast to the chaos in her head, with its muted tones, queen-sized four-poster bed, and antique tables. The floor-length curtains matched the duvet, offering an elegant but comforting atmosphere.

Setting her journal aside, she scanned the room, but her

mind was elsewhere—on the impossible, and the hauntingly familiar face of a man who shouldn't exist.

Her host's words repeated over and over in her mind.

Did the woman truly believe her ancestor to be alive? Was Edith convinced that he'd survived more than three hundred years trapped in a supposed enchantment?

The assignment could prove to be more difficult than she expected. She would help, but perhaps not in the way Edith expected.

That Tristan McRainey lingered in this world meant he had yet to accept he was dead and therefore was a restless spirit. It was her duty to help wayward spirits, and she would do just that.

Once she helped the dead man move on to the next plane, then she'd have to explain to Edith that it was not possible to bring the dead back to the land of the living.

Still considering everything they spoke about, she went to the small but well-appointed bathroom and made quick work of washing her face and brushing her teeth.

The entire time, Tristan's searching gaze formed in her mind. She'd have to hand it to Edith, the spirit was certainly compelling. Not only was he visibly emotional, but somehow he was strong enough to communicate with her.

Gwen let out a breath. She was tired, had only been in Scotland a pair of days, which meant it wasn't the time to put full trust in anything she may have perceived.

Finally, with a book in hand, she slid into the plush bed hoping to read until sleepy. Unfortunately, her mind would not settle, thoughts swirling in her head until she gave up and put the book down.

It wasn't uncommon that she get excited at the prospect of a new assignment. She lived for the times when it was possible to get away from the drudgery of her nine-to-five job at a publishing company and head out to faraway places like Scotland to see about pesky apparitions.

For some reason, thinking of the ghost of Tristan as an apparition felt wrong, but it was the truth.

Although most of her work was exciting and interesting, this one would certainly be one of the most interesting.

ONCE AGAIN SHE pulled out her notes, considering how for several hours Edith had regaled Gwen with an elaborate tale, confiding in her the entirety of the McRainey family legend regarding Tristan McRainey. She'd enthralled her, telling Gwen an account that consisted of conquests, wizards, and enchantments. If Gwen didn't know any better, she'd call the woman crazy for believing in the fairy tale.

Yet.

Edith believed every bit of it to be true and Gwen wished deeply that she could also believe it, because it was a sad, but magical tale.

Gwen could not make herself believe Edith was crazy. Maybe, after hearing the story of the enchanted knights all her life, the woman grew up believing Tristan McRainey was alive and truly imprisoned in an alter-world.

For a long moment Gwen studied the ceiling. How would Edith take the news that he was a ghost? Better yet, how to explain it in a way without making the woman upset.

Tristan McRainey and his men had undoubtedly died

over three hundred years ago. The story of the five brave knights captured by a wizard was someone's notion after they'd disappeared. Perhaps the story had helped the grieving families cope with the loss of their men.

Gwen had to admit that after seeing the man for the second time since arriving, she herself almost believed him to be real, not a ghost. The apparition had been so clear, the emotions that he projected so tangible.

The ornate lamp on the bedside table flickered and the bulbs went out darkening the room. Gwen didn't bother getting up, she'd already decided reading was out of the question tonight. Tomorrow she'd ask Edith for a replacement light bulb.

The apparition's piercing sea-green eyes formed in her mind. They were truly an astonishing color, the likes of which she'd never seen before. Who had Tristan McRainey been? She sighed. They didn't make men like that anymore.

So much masculine power emanated from him. Just the way he carried himself, with authority, an assurance that came from being a true alpha male, the leader of his clan. Good-looking too—the man was a total hottie.

Gwen closed her eyes and pictured life so long ago. What had his life been like all those years ago, when he'd lived there in Scotland during the time of honorable knights? No doubt women flocked to him.

The intensity of Tristan McRainey alone was a turn-on.

What if he was really trapped in an enchantment?

If for some unimaginable reason it was true, then Gwen would be totally out of her element. Not by a bit, but by miles, hundreds of miles.

Although her mother, Iona, had taught her and her two sisters many spells and protection wards, Gwen didn't recall that she'd ever mentioned enchantments.

"Dear Lord, why am I here?" Gwen grumbled aloud.

"You are here to free me."

The sound of the deep voice jerked her out of her thoughts, and she sprang up, squinting into the darkness.

"W-where are you?" she stammered, looking around the room, her eyes wide. Moonlight gave only a bit of light.

Thinking it was best to face the apparition on her feet, Gwen slid to the edge of the mattress. In her haste to climb out of the bed she got tangled up in the sheets, the damn things wrapped tighter around her legs when she tried to pull them off.

Finally, all she managed to do was get one leg free.

"Show yourself," she hissed toward the corner where a shadow moved.

A ghost speaking to her was not an unusual occurrence. It happened to her all the time. And yet the tingle of apprehension at her nape was unwelcome.

The shadow moved closer, and Gwen followed its movements, subconsciously rubbing her arms. When he finally moved into the light of a moonbeam that filtered from in between the curtains, her lips parted, and she lost the ability to speak.

This time Tristan McRainey dressed differently. He wore a white shirt, open to his waist, showcasing his ripped chest and a serious six-pack. This was definitely a good-looking man... ghost.

Chestnut-brown hair, pulled back with a strap, accentuated the hard lines of his face. Again, his penetrating gaze rested on her.

She continued to study him. His lips were full, sensuous. The width of his shoulders and lean waist, not to mention his stature of at least six-foot-three, made him an enticing sight. That and the muscular legs, so defined by his tight-fitting leather breeches and the calf-high leather boots, didn't hurt the look.

Her attention shifted to his hand. He held a broadsword this time and seemed agitated as if holding back his temper.

"Why do you think I can free you?" Gwen whispered, looking straight into his eyes, checking for the ghostly telltale sign of transparency. He was as solid as she was.

Crap, what was he?

"Because I am Tristan McRainey and ye are an enchantress," he replied, shocking her. "I've been waiting for ye to come. And finally, ye came and ye summoned me."

The ghost cocked his head to the side, his gaze roaming over her. She followed his line of vision to find his eyes locked on her chest, exactly where her top gaped open, exposing a large portion of her breasts. She grabbed the blankets up to cover herself.

"I am no enchantress," Gwen said, frowning at him. "And I didn't summon you." Why was she arguing with a ghost? What she had to do was to begin to introduce to him the idea that he was trapped between planes. Entice him to move to the other side.

He lifted an eyebrow as if amused, and this time his gaze slid at a leisurely pace down her exposed leg. She huffed before sliding her leg under the blankets and glaring at the oversexed ghost.

"What kind of a ghost are you anyway? Stop looking at me that way."

He continued to study the space where her leg slid under the blanket. "Pity. Ye should not hide such beauty." He spoke slowly, as if ensuring she understood every word. "I am not a ghost. I am Lord Tristan McRainey, the laird of this land. Hundreds of years ago, when on our way to meet with an assembly of knights, four men and I were enchanted by a powerful wizard. I'm to be released by you."

"Assembly... as in some sort of round table?" Gwen stammered, her eyes wide. She scrambled to remember the story of King Arthur's knights. It was fictional, but there wasn't any other grouping of knights she could think of.

"An assembly called by King James," Tristan clarified.

"Right." Gwen replied slowly. She'd play along and hopefully gain his trust so that he'd be more amenable to her suggestions later. "Who enchanted you?"

"Meliot. A wizard with great power. He is a dark relation of Merlin's," Tristan's ghost replied, taking a step closer.

This time she wanted to laugh. Merlin was definitely not real.

"Why aren't you disappearing this time?" She asked him, changing the subject and prompting him to stop his advance. She almost wished she'd not spoken. If anything, Gwen wanted to touch him to find out if indeed he was something quite different than a ghost.

"I have been able to will myself inside the keep more often and for longer periods since ye arrived," he answered, taking another step toward her. "Ye are a vera powerful enchantress."

"No, I'm not," Gwen squeaked. "You are mistaken."

He'd finally reached her bed, and she stared at the broadsword he still held. "Wh-what are you going to do with that sword?"

He faltered, his gaze snapping down to the weapon. A frown formed on his brow, as if he'd forgotten he held it. He grimaced and almost looked embarrassed at scaring her.

"I meant no harm, I was practicing. Prior to feeling the pull to come to ye," Tristan explained, sliding the sword into a strap of some type at his hip. When he looked at her again, his intense demeanor returned. "Ye must free me at once."

Gwen gave him a droll look and decided to play along. "Maybe you could ask more nicely? I am going to try my best. But I must admit, I've never broken enchantments. I have no idea how to start."

The intensity in his eyes at her words unsettled her. The gold specks in the sea of green seemed to flicker.

Slowly, he reached out and touched her arm, his face tight in concentration. It was as if it took a lot of effort to control his movements. His fingers slid unhurriedly down her arm. His warm fingertips traced a path leaving a trail of heat that she'd not felt in a long time. A ghost had never touched her before—well, not like this.

Sure, ghosts had passed through her, attempted to possess her and once a poltergeist shoved her across a room, but all of them felt cold, frigid. Tristan's touch was warm, human, and her reaction to it much too real.

She finally reacted and scooted away from his hand. "Can

you give me some idea as to what I am to do?" Gwen gave him her best 'back off' look and waited for him to reply.

Her eyes widened at noticing a change in the color of his eyes. They'd darkened, emerald green now. Hesitantly she lowered her gaze to his mid-section.

The ghost was aroused!

Forcing her gaze away, she spoke in what she hoped was a calm, unfazed manner. "Can you give me an idea about where I'm supposed to start? You know, with this enchantment. How can I help you, Tristan?" She repeated.

He didn't reply, instead leaned in closer. She froze. Was the apparition going to kiss her?

For an inexplicable reason, she hoped so.

Chapter Three

Despite the fog in his head, Tristan caught himself and moved away from the gorgeous woman in the bed.

What was he doing? This was certainly not the time to attempt to seduce a woman. For starters, he wasn't sure he'd be able to remain in the current realm much longer, and secondly... he had more important things to consider.

His freedom for instance.

How long since he'd been with a woman, a beautiful one like the one who watched him with interest? Did he even remember what it felt like to hold someone? How long since he'd been thoroughly spent, buried deep inside a vixen like the one before him now? He dared not try to ponder it any longer.

A part of him he thought long dormant awakened. Was it hope? By the hammering of his heart underneath his breast, just the possibility was almost more than he could bear.

He looked down at the enchantress who eyed him in

return with suspicion. He was willing to bet the woman didn't realize what an enticing sight she made. If not for his current state, he would not hesitate to join her in the bed, kiss her until she gave in, and then make love to her for hours.

Would she enjoy his touch?

She was lovely, her rumpled midnight-black hair cascading down her back, a curtain of silken tresses, like velvet fabric it swayed each time she moved. It took all his strength to stop from reaching and wrapping his fingers around it.

Hands fisted, he stalked back to the window, his favorite element of each room. Windows served as portals where he could look outside and catch glimpses of the changes that had transpired through the years.

Hundreds of years of trials and captivity, and now at last he had hope.

Before he could begin to explain the rules of breaking his enchantment, the strong pull jerked at him. Time was up and he had to return.

In a matter of minutes the pull would become too strong, and he'd not be able to resist and be forced to return to the alter-world.

Tristan rushed back to the bed. Without thinking, he grabbed her shoulders and pulled the surprised woman to him.

His mouth covered hers.

Her gasp the only invitation he needed. Driving his tongue deep into her mouth, he almost collapsed on weakened legs from her taste. Mint intermingled with her natural flavor, reminding him of the wild fragrant plants that grew on the Scottish countryside.

Too long. So many years, waiting for this moment. How he missed women, their touch, their scent, and their taste. The kiss became savage, hungry, and passionate. Tristan feared he'd lose control, his craving barely satisfied. For a split second he wondered if he hurt her, but as if on cue, she moaned and wrapped her arms around his shoulders, her hands traveling to his upper arms to pull him closer. The feel of her breasts pressed against him was his undoing, he groaned at the intensity of the moment.

No longer in control, his hands slid to the small of her back. The feel of her silky hair between his fingers almost brought him to his knees, then the pull became too strong, and he could not fight it.

"No," she whispered as he vanished.

TRISTAN HIT THE GROUND HARD, his body convulsed in agony. Each time he moved between planes and returned to the alter-world, the pain was excruciating. He writhed from the torture, a feeling like that of muscles peeling away from bones. Clenching his jaw to keep from screaming, he could not stop the tears that flowed down his face. A firm hand on his shoulder instantly calmed the pain, until finally the hurting subsided, becoming bearable.

Still it took a few moments before he could breathe normally, and Tristan opened his eyes. The healer maintained a close eye on him, his hand still gripping his shoulder.

Prior to entering the enchantment, a powerful enchantress gifted each knight with an amulet and a special power.

Niall, the knight who knelt beside Tristan, received the gift of healing, which came in handy. Especially after moving between worlds.

"My gratitude, Niall." Tristan sat up, allowing his head to flop forward until his chin rested on his chest. He managed to lift his hand, and Niall pulled him to his feet.

"Ye were gone too long this time. Ye are vera weak." The dark Irishman gave him a worried look. "Shall I carry ye? The others await us inside. We had a wee bit of trouble while ye were gone."

That being the most he'd heard Niall say in a long time, Tristan didn't question him further.

He shook his head, the action costing him when a dizzy spell hit. "No need to carry me, I can make it."

Nail gave him a dubious look and walked away without another word.

Tristan followed him at a slower pace toward a large stone castle where they lived, most of the time, sometimes for years, without incident or challenges.

Both men continuously scanned the surrounding area. They knew better than to be at ease. Their captor didn't allow for a peaceful existence.

"What kind of trouble, Niall?" Not able to restrain his curiosity, Tristan asked his friend when he caught up to him.

Niall motioned with his right hand for him to pick up the pace and they jogged toward the keep. The Irishman looked skyward and scanned the vast expanse.

Finally he pinned him with one of his usual annoyed looks.

Niall MacTavish, one of Scotland's best lancers, had won many a joust in his lifetime. Back then, he seemed to live for the accolades of winning the many competitions but once off the field he reverted to his norm, a silent solitary man.

Already a quiet male, since coming to the alter-world, Niall had become even more sullen and withdrawn, rarely joining them for meals, even less for conversations.

"Liam will explain," Niall finally replied, as they continued on into the keep.

A rumble from the purple-hued sky alerted them to the possibility of rain. In this realm, rain could be anything from water and ice to fire, so they hurried inside to the security afforded by the solid grey stone walls of their home.

As soon as Niall and Tristan were inside, hail began falling, pelting the roof, the sounds of it echoing throughout.

Used to it, Tristan ignored the noisy bangs. He trusted that the youngest knight, Padraig's, magical wards were strong against the assault. Besides, the matter at hand seemed quite serious, by the stoic faces of the other men inside the main room.

The gloomy chamber, lit with magic torches and a vivid fire from the enormous fireplace, relieved Tristan's chill.

Three men sat around a large plain wooden table where they took their meals. They'd kept certain habits such as sitting together and sharing meals, as a way of staying in touch with their humanity.

He and Niall joined the men at the table.

The four men had become his family since having been spellbound together for centuries.

Besides the morose Niall, there was Padraig Clarre, a young, brash, humorous Scottish warrior, the youth of the group who kept them entertained with his antics and magic tricks.

Then there was Tristan's childhood friend, a Scottish laird, Gavin Campbell. His unrivaled beauty had always made it impossible for anyone that came upon him not to gawk. Thankfully, over the many years, he and the others in the room were immune to the man's beauty. Gavin, who had the power of seduction, rarely had occasion to use his gift in the alter-world. A fact he repeatedly insisted was a gift in itself.

The fourth man was Liam Murray, an English knight, whom they'd come upon on the fate-filled day they'd been bound to the enchantment. Murray's gift of foresight proved to be almost as valuable as Niall's healing during their many travails.

The men had endured much during the years in the alter-world as they were constantly tested by different challenges. They'd been attacked by dragons, soulless warriors, and individually thrown into whatever surreal torment the evil mind of the wizard Meliot conjured.

As a result, the men had become closer than brothers. After so many trials and seeing each other at their worst, it was doubtful they could ever find any other person who could ever come close to breaching their bond.

Tristan met each of their gazes before sitting, reassured when not one of them averted their eyes.

Liam leaned forward from the head of the table. Lord Liam Murray was of Norse ancestry, evident by his piercing ice-blue eyes and almost white-blonde hair, which he kept short, barely past his nape. The knight looked around the room before speaking, as if measuring his words. "The day ye left we were attacked."

Astounded, Tristan's eyes widened. "How long was I gone?" That time moved differently on the two planes made timekeeping difficult for them while leaping. Although time seemed to move at a normal rate in the alter-world, when they went to current time, it moved faster.

"Two days," Gavin told him.

He'd thought to have been gone less than an hour, if that. But the fact that, in this plane, he'd been gone so much longer didn't surprise him. Nothing did anymore.

Tristan looked back to Liam. "Attacked how? Were ye caught outside? Were they able to enter the keep?"

"A group of centaurs and a couple Minotaur attacked before we could make it back inside, after escorting ye out to leap," Liam replied.

Minotaur were exceptionally strong, but not usually a deathly threat when in small numbers. "There were about twenty centaurs," Padraig added shaking his head.

Tristan now noticed bruises and some bandages. Gavin sported a nasty gash on his jaw that was already healing. Padraig's left eye was slightly swollen, his bottom lip split, and Liam's right hand was wrapped in bandages.

It seemed Niall had been busy.

Liam spoke again after allowing Tristan to look about the room, pride in his voice. "Of course, we were able to defend ourselves and managed to kill more than half before making it back to the keep."

"A missive was nailed to the front door when we reached it." Gavin handed Tristan a piece of rolled parchment.

The parchment crackled as Tristan unrolled it, everyone's eyes landed on him as he read the words.

"Betrayal will come. Lord McRainey will turn against all of ye in his quest for freedom. He will gain his freedom at the expense of yours. Be warned."

Tristan slammed his fist on the tabletop and jumped to his feet, his chair falling behind him. "I will never betray any of you and I will not leave unless we all leave together. That is my oath."

Padraig, who'd sat next to him, stood as well and placed his hand on Tristan's shoulder. "We don't doubt ye Tristan. But ye cannot make such an oath."

The young knight looked around the room at the other men. "Ye know the rules of the enchantment. We can only leave one at a time, unless by some chance two of our fates are linked. Each of us will have a different quest, a different enchantress, and a different outcome."

"Of course, this could be Meliot's way to dissuade ye from seeking the enchantress that will free us," Gavin replied, his golden gaze meeting his. "And since the rules don't allow for us to know what is true and what is not..." He didn't finish, turning toward the fire.

"To hell with this place and its damned rules," Tristan exclaimed. "Why do we even try? Everything in this accursed place has been and will always be a lie. If this enchantress manages to get past Meliot's spell binding me here, I have little doubt another binding of some sort will take its place."

He stormed from the room tired of all the tricks and rules and even more exhausted by the hope that had dared to flicker within him.

As he walked away, he overheard Padraig chuckle, "We didn't even get to ask him about his trip."

He hesitated in the hallway, trying to decide if he needed to return to the room. Truth be told, he shouldn't have lost his temper. It wasn't their fault. They, like him, went through the same experience.

"Be silent, Paddy," Liam admonished the young knight. "More than we can imagine is in store for Tristan."

Liam, who had the gift of foresight, continued. "I only hope this lass is as strong as he needs her to be."

Chapter Four

Derrick McRainey, Edith's nephew, arrived early the next the morning. Gwen and Edith had barely sat down to breakfast when he walked through the doorway and paused just inside, his lips curving in greeting.

Allowing her gaze to take in the man's appearance, which he seemed to be expecting, Gwen couldn't help but acknowledge that the McRainey genes were definitely passed down to Derrick.

The dark-haired man stood well over six feet tall, was broad-shouldered with an athletic physique. No wonder he'd had success as a rich playboy, if social media was any indicator.

"Aunt Edith, you look well. May I join you for breakfast?" he asked. Then he turned to Gwen. "Good morning, miss." His dark eyes sparkled mischievously at her.

"Good morning," both women replied.

Edith turned her face up when he neared and kissed her

cheek. Then she extended her hand, motioning to the chair opposite Gwen's. "Derrick, please join us."

She regarded her nephew with a cool smile and was silent for a moment, then seemed to gain her composure. "This is Gwyneth Lockhart, the professional ghost medium I hired to see about Tristan McRainey."

The same maid who'd brought tea the day before served Derrick his breakfast. He waited until the young woman left before speaking to Gwen.

"I trust you find the estate to your liking, Miss Lockhart. The lands are beautiful are they not?" He studied her closely without blinking, the intensity reminding her of the experience with another McRainey the night before.

"Oh yes, it's quite lovely, and please, call me Gwen," Gwen replied instantly, feeling disconcerted by the man. "I'm not here as a guest—I'm employed by your aunt."

"Of course you're a guest, dear. My guest," Edith replied smiling warmly, before speaking to her nephew. "Miss Lockhart is not only wonderful company, but she has already met our elusive Lord."

Derrick visibly tensed, and his raised eyebrows almost disappeared into his perfectly styled hair. "What? Do you mean you've seen the ghost?"

Before she could reply, he cut her off. "Did he speak to you?"

At a peculiar tingle on her nape, she decided not to tell all. Not yet. "I got a quick glimpse of someone, an apparition, in the sitting room. And no, he didn't speak."

"Ah, so it was a male... er... apparition then?" Derrick persisted. "And you assume it was Lord Tristan McRainey?"

"Oh yes, dear," Edith interrupted. "I told her it must be him, since I can't recall any other ghost ever being seen here."

Earlier, Gwen had learned from Edith that throughout the years, different family members spotted the Lord on occasion, usually by a window and always peering out.

Derrick waited as the maid reentered to refresh their tea. He flashed the young woman a devilish smile, seeming to enjoy her blush. Gwen followed the interaction, noticing the girl glancing back at Lord Derrick before exiting. No doubt one of many young women who'd fallen for his charms.

Edith cleared her throat delicately, getting her nephew's attention. "Derrick, did you bring the pictures of Tristan? The large portrait in the hallway east of the sitting room has gone missing." Her voice pitched at the last grief-stricken word. "I can't believe I didn't notice it was gone."

"Aunt Edith, I'm sure I told you. The portrait is in Edinburgh. An art expert is cleaning it and ensuring it's properly protected from the elements," Derrick told his aunt, his voice taking on a sugary tone.

A slow flush covered Edith's face, her demeanor shifting. With purpose, she put her fork down and glared at her nephew. "Why Derrick McRainey, you certainly did not inform me of such a thing. I would have flatly refused that type of request. The portrait is not to be removed from the property for any reason. It's against Tristan McRainey's wishes. A local art expert stops by on occasion to care for it."

Feeling like an intruder, Gwen shifted in her seat. At the same time, she couldn't wait to hear the arrogant man's reply. His eyes met hers briefly, almost as if hearing her thoughts.

The bland look he gave his aunt betrayed his words. "I

did not mean to distress you Aunt Edith. I will have the portrait returned at once. Or better yet, I will be traveling to Edinburgh in a few days. I will pick it up from the art expert and will personally deliver it upon my return. My intentions are good, I assure you. I am ensuring proper care of the estate property, prior to the changes coming about."

"Changes?" Gwen wished she could retract the question, but the word hung in the already heavy air. "I'm sorry—it's probably none of my business."

"On the contrary dear," Edith gave her a tight smile. "Upon my death, my nephew will inherit the McRainey estate, since there are no female McRaineys left in the direct family line after me."

Her smile faded as she looked toward the sitting room. "He plans to transform our home into a public attraction."

"Aunt Edith!" Derrick exclaimed his face reddening. "A luxury hotel and exclusive golf resort is far from a 'public attraction,' as you insist on calling it."

Gwen gasped, not sure why the thought of it infuriated her as well. The house shouldn't mean anything to her. Nonetheless, before she could squelch her emotions, the table shook violently, causing some of the dishes to fly up and land in a noisy concerto of rattles and clangs.

After his initial shock, Derrick McRainey turned to her, one brow raised, his expression condescending. "I assume your telekinetic abilities come in handy in your profession as a ghost expeller."

Gwen flushed, hating her inability to control her erratic powers when upset. "I apologize. I didn't mean to do that. I'm not sure why I even reacted."

Disconcerted, she pushed away from the table. "I'm sorry, Edith. I need to lie down for a bit. May I please look at the pictures later?"

Elation played on Edith's face; she seemed excited to learn of Gwen's abilities. "Of course, of course, dear, please go rest. Derrick and I have much to discuss. He will be staying for a couple of days."

Glad to escape, Gwen hurried up the stairs, not slowing until closing the door behind her. Her mother would be mortified if she learned of her failure to control her abilities.

While growing up in their large antebellum house south of Atlanta, every evening she and her sisters, Sabrina and Tammie, would sit around the kitchen table, while their mother prepared dinner.

Each girl took turns practicing using her abilities while their mother looked on. A spoon would wiggle in the air in front of Gwen as she tried to get it to dip into a cup of milk, more times than not ending with milk splashed all over her face, her sisters giggling at her efforts.

Over time, all of their abilities became stronger and more controllable. For the most part Gwen rarely lost any control. It was only when she became very upset that her powers became erratic.

In this instance, it made little sense. What happened to the McRainey property wasn't any concern of hers. At least it shouldn't have been. And yet, the thought of the beautiful castle becoming a public place did feel almost sacrilegious. She could certainly relate to Edith's feelings about it.

Chapter Five

Tristan paced restlessly back and forth in his chamber, his soft leather boots soundless on the stone floor. It was times like these, when he needed nothing more than to be on horseback riding at breakneck speed across open fields with no particular destination, that he abhorred the imprisonment the most.

Would he finally be free?

He pondered the terms of breaking his enchantment. It would be more difficult than any quest.

First, he was to find the enchantress whose presence would be a strong call to him. There was little doubt in his mind the raven-haired beauty was she.

Secondly, the enchantress would have to not only cast a specific spell, but she must fall in love with him, and then be willing to give up something very dear to her in order for him to be freed.

The influence to go to his home had been irresistible as soon as Gwyneth Lockhart had arrived.

His senses had changed and become razor sharp the moment she'd arrived in Scotland. Tristan's only worry now—to help her find the specific spell. He didn't foresee any problem with the third and fourth part.

Women had always fallen in love with him and professed their undying devotion to him when he'd been the Laird McRainey. And a woman in love was always more than willing to sacrifice anything for the man she loved.

He pulled the window covering back and studied the familiar landscape. A dense forest surrounded their keep. The thick woods hid deadly creatures, waiting for one of them to venture too close. Beyond the forest lay a wide expanse of land, Atlandia, a frozen arctic tundra, governed by royals who kept Meliot in line, protecting their people from peril at the hands of the evil wizard.

Two suns blazed on most days; right now one was setting, leaving the other behind to battle it out with the two moons rising on the opposite horizon. The sunset gave the landscape a dark-red hue, almost earthlike. The temperature in this alter-world was moderate at the moment. Daily, the weather could range from freezing to inferno. Seasons did not exist in this world.

They'd not had to wonder who'd sent the missive. It had to be from Meliot, always sowing discord.

Although he was sure the others didn't believe he'd ever betray them, he wasn't reassured. He'd gotten to know their captor well enough to suspect a catch of some kind. If the wizard had become concerned enough to cast doubt, there must be a good chance this might be his moment to defeat the enchantment.

Tristan turned away from the window, for the first time in a very long-time feeling anticipation for what lay ahead. The contemplation ended abruptly, when two arrows flew through the narrow window, one sinking into his lower back, the other into his right shoulder.

It took a few beats before the pain penetrated his brain and he fell to his knees, calling for the others.

Cursed centaurs, the only ones with good enough skill to shoot an arrow with such accuracy at a long distance, past Padraig's spells, through the small window and still hit their target. Tristan fell forward hearing the fast footsteps of his friends coming to his assistance.

MOMENTS LATER, he gritted his teeth and bit into a piece of leather while Niall pushed the second arrow through the flesh of his shoulder and broke it off. The searing pain was followed by Niall's healing power flooding him, the warmth soothing away the pain.

"You won't be able to travel to the other world anytime soon. The wounds may reopen," Niall told him, his expression grim.

"Do not try to stop me. I must continue this."

Niall nodded and looked away.

The others had yet to seem relieved. They wished for him to remain healthy enough to continue to travel to current time.

Their collective hope lay in the chance that, once his enchantment broke, it would start a chain reaction making it easier for them to be freed as well. Once on the other side, he would search for their enchantresses, not rest until they were all free.

There was no choice. He had to go, leap to present time Scotland and see the enchantress again. Being trapped here without hope would lead them all to madness.

For a moment Tristan and Niall locked gazes, communicating without words. Finally Niall let out a heavy sigh.

"I will heal your injuries as best I can and let's hope it holds."

Tristan lay back allowing Niall's healing energy to flow through him. He closed his eyes until he heard footsteps enter.

Gavin stepped in, the large Scot having to duck to not bump his head in the doorway. Golden eyes watched as Niall healed him, a pensive expression on his face.

"When are ye planning to go again? Perhaps it's best if ye wait for the wounds to heal."

Having known Gavin since childhood, it was obvious to him something bothered his friend.

"What troubles you, Gavin?" Tristan asked. Enjoying the flow of warmth Niall's healing brought, he closed his eyes again.

"The last time ye went, it was for too long. If for some unknown reason it becomes impossible for ye to return, remember that you will begin to age at a very rapid rate. Do not take that chance, Tristan." The hoarseness in Gavin's voice touched him. He opened his eyes, as Niall finished healing him.

Watching the quiet man leave, he got up and pulled on a tunic.

"I will pay heed to your concerns, Gavin, but I must go. Our freedom depends on it. It is only from the other side that I can work to find the other enchantresses and help the rest of ye." Absently, he laid a hand over his wounded shoulder. "Is something else amiss?"

Gavin's worry-filled eyes met his. "Nay."

His friend was afraid, not of the dangers they faced every day, not of death, but of getting his hopes up, only to be disappointed again. Tristan allowed the lie.

"Come, let's go downstairs and join the others."

Chapter Six

"I trust you are feeling better, Miss Lockhart." Derrick McRainey met Gwen at the bottom of the stairs as she descended from a short nap, his hand outstretched. She accepted his assistance, and when their hands touched, a strange stirring shook her. If he noticed her slight flinch, he didn't give any indication of it.

Entering the sitting room, she glanced about. They were alone. Edith must have gone out.

After he motioned to a narrow couch, Gwen sat, and Derrick joined her. The proximity of the man was a bit too familiar, their knees almost touching.

When he turned to open a briefcase on the table in front of them, she was able to shift away as much as she could without it being obvious.

"This photograph of Tristan McRainey's portrait was kept at my mother's house in case of a fire, for insurance purposes, of course," he told her, pulling out the picture and handing it to her.

Gwen's heart skipped seeing the photo. It was the apparition. The man who'd come to her had been Tristan McRainey.

She schooled her features, keeping her expression purposely blank as she studied the picture. Tristan stood beside a huge black stallion, his eyes looking to the distance, his features set impatiently, as if hating to be still. In the portrait, his hair was longer than the two times she'd seen him, flowing past his shoulders, a thick mass of dark brown waves. The way he held the hilt of his sword was familiar to her, his fist relaxed on it.

Even in the photograph, his good looks were hard to ignore. The man was gorgeous.

"Speechless, Miss Lockhart?" Derrick asked her, his voice tight. "Attracted to a dead man?"

Gwen fought not to roll her eyes at him, she arched an eyebrow at him. "Threatened by a dead man, Lord McRainey?"

"Touché."

She shrugged. "According to your aunt, he is very much alive." Gwen lifted her eyes from the picture in her hand to meet Derrick's.

He gave her a droll look. "I cannot fathom how a woman like Aunt Edith can believe such nonsense."

"I take it you don't believe that he is trapped in an enchantment"

"Not at all."

She studied him as he began to rummage through the briefcase. His aristocratic demeanor did not distract from his looks. Derrick had definitely inherited his height and physique from the McRainey side of the family. Unlike Tristan, Derrick was fair, with light brown hair that barely touched the collar of his shirt. When he turned to hand her a miniature portrait, she noted that his eyes were dark brown, not green like his ancestor's. They seemed too dark for his coloring, his penetrating gaze unsettling.

"This miniature was done for his future wife. According to family legend, he killed her before they could marry." He watched for a reaction.

Gwen gasped, reaching for the miniature slowly. "Why did he kill her?"

Derrick shrugged one shoulder dismissively. "If one is to believe those things, it's said that he killed her after he caught her consorting with his worst enemy. Some local man."

Gwen didn't reply. She studied the miniature, this time a younger Tristan. He looked to be barely a man, perhaps nineteen, however he did not have the carefree expression of youth. Instead, his brow remained pinched. He definitely did not like having his portrait done. She held on to the miniature and the photograph. "Can I keep these?"

"Of course. I have another copy of the photograph. The miniature is very old, so take care with it."

He gave her a questioning look. "Well? Is he the same man that appeared to you yesterday?"

For an inexplicable reason Gwen did not feel inclined to trust Derrick. She'd been hired by Edith and would much rather talk to her first. "I'm not sure. The apparition was hazy, translucent almost. I hope when he appears again I will be able to get a better look and compare him to these." She looked down at the miniature on her lap to avoid his eyes.

"Very well." Derrick didn't seem altogether convinced; he watched her closely for a moment before continuing. "Would you like a tour of the lands? I would like to show you the estate and perhaps take you into town—you'll enjoy the shops there."

Gwen hesitated, unsettled by his invitation. "Will Edith be joining us?"

"She's already in town. We'll probably run into her there."

DESPITE HER MISGIVINGS, Gwen enjoyed the tour of the McRainey lands with Derrick more than she expected. He proved to be an excellent tour guide, pride in the family estate evident in his voice, a smile constantly playing on his lips as he described his childhood there. They stopped many times as he regaled her with stories of his youth and the history of specific areas and buildings.

Derrick drove slowly stopping frequently to point out different flora native to the land. He astounded her with his knowledge of it.

Finally, they stopped atop a small hill, and he climbed from the vehicle, making it obvious she was to do the same.

When she stood to look out, he waited in silence, allowing her to take in the view. She looked down to the large, proud, grey stonewalled home, the lavish gardens surrounding it, and the aged but well-kept stables. She couldn't help but wonder. How different was it from when Tristan McRainey lived there so many years earlier?

Pointing toward the ocean, Derrick got her attention. "Over there, the large area between the stream and the shoreline is the perfect setting for a championship golf course." He didn't wait for her opinion, but instead pointed in another direction. "We'll build new stables in this area below to allow plenty of room for riding trails into the wooded area and along the opposite bank of the creek." The expectant look on his face told her, he wanted a reply this time.

"The land is beautiful. You'll have to clear a lot of trees for a golf course," she told him, looking towards the area he'd pointed to earlier. "I'm always saddened when trees are cut down, the victims of modernization." She sighed and looked toward the stables. "I love the old stables; they are very old are they not? Can't you just fix them?"

"Yes." Derrick's answer was terse. "But they're hundreds of years old and require constant repairs."

His face brightened as he motioned toward the home. "The main house will only require minor upgrades, as it must remain true to its history. To attract the right people, of course."

"Of course," Gwen replied, a forced smile on her face. What did he mean by "minor upgrades?"

Derrick stepped closer, abruptly changing the topic of conversation, catching her off guard. "You are a beautiful woman, Miss Lockhart. Your coloring is quite unusual. Very appealing." His dark eyes lingered on her lips just a bit too long for comfort.

With a step back, she hid her uneasiness by turning back

to the view. "My father is Native American. I get my olive skin and black hair from him."

"Ah." He moved closer again, a slight curve to his lips. "Which tribe?"

Damn it, he was trying to seduce her! "Choctaw... you've probably never heard of them."

"I have. I studied in America—they are traditionally from the southeastern portion of the United States," he said, reaching to touch her hair. "Lovely."

It wasn't anything new. Gwyneth knew she was an attractive woman. Through the years she'd become proficient at avoiding men's advances. Pretending not to notice his hand on her hair, she swung away and headed toward his car.

"We better get a move on. I am anxious to see the Culross. We can't be too long. I really do have to get back here to work."

The drive into the small town gave her another opportunity to study the lush landscape of Scotland. The shades of green pulled at her heartstrings, impressing upon her how easy it would be to fall in love with the country.

When they arrived at the small town on the shores of Fife of Furth, the car bounced along the narrow cobblestone road until Derrick found a parking spot and pulled into it.

"This town is so pretty," Gwen exclaimed, watching a woman pushing a stroller, shopping bags hanging from it, a small dog trotting alongside.

"Look at that," She pointed out a small white building with a shingle hanging on the exterior wall. "That's City Hall? How quaint is that!" Derrick nodded, smiling at her enthusiasm.

They walked to a café marked with a kettle-shaped sign that read *Bessie's Café*. The interior was awash in white with wooden crossbeams overhead. Gwen took in the details, unable to keep from grinning. What was it about this country that every place brought delight?

Chapter Seven

During lunch, Derrick received a call from his office, regarding an urgent matter. He'd reluctantly left to attend to the issue.

It gave Gwen an opportunity to get to know Edith better and get the gist of the woman's thinking. No matter how hard she tried to find something *off* about the older woman, she couldn't find any fault with her hostess.

After a delightful lunch of soup, scones, and tea, Edith insisted on giving Gwen a tour of the town. They popped into a pottery shop next door, and Gwen picked up a few things before they drove back to the Dunimarle in Edith's car.

Once in her room, Gwen went through her purchases and hung up a sweater she'd purchased. The day turned out to be quite delightful, so much so that she'd almost forgotten her reason for being in Scotland was to work and not a holiday.

After putting things away, she took a hot shower, planning to slip into warm pajamas for the evening. She'd make a pot of tea and settle in with a good book.

Her plan was to stay up most of the night to keep an eye out for Tristan's ghost. Hopefully the Laird would appear, and she'd be able to get more information from him. The more she thought about it, he had to be some sort of poltergeist. Although a bit trickier, they could still be guided to move on.

Despite how real he'd seemed and the fact she could physically touch him, she had to remain strong against the strange pull she felt toward him. It was utterly ridiculous to be attracted to a ghost. For someone like her, a professional medium, it was also embarrassing.

In the bathroom, Gwen studied her reflection and wondered if Tristan McRainey would try to touch her again? She ran a comb through her wet hair, thinking of his kiss. It had been so real. What was stranger was the fact that she'd smelled him. A very rare occurrence indeed. His lips had been warm, not the usual cold touch of the deceased, and the heady scent of him, a mixture of pine and outdoors, was something she'd never experienced.

A shiver went up her spine. This was ridiculous. She was a professional, not some Twilight teen fan who hoped to be romanced by a cute dead guy. *Her job was to help Tristan McRainey move on, to rid this home of the ghost, and then return home and start a new job. No matter how strong his ties to this world, he was only an apparition.*

With a firm nod, she felt more assured, she'd set her mind

straight. Now, time to find those pajamas and await the appearance of a dead man.

Every bit of the pep talk she'd just given herself flew out the window when she turned out of the bathroom and looked to the bed. Gwen stopped short.

The ghost... *apparition* was on his side, atop the coverlet, looking very much at home.

Her mouth fell open, but no words came out. What could she say? How was it possible for this... whatever he was... to be so real that his body made indentations on the mattress. Tunic gaped open at the neck, she spied a light sprinkling of hair. Everything about him was temptation.

"Hallo, Gwyneth." His smooth voice melted over her like a warm blanket. "I have been waiting for you."

The towel she'd wrapped around herself suddenly seemed to shrink under his scrutiny. Gwen fidgeted and eyed her pajamas on the bed next to him.

"Err, give me a minute." She went as close to him as she dared and reached for the clothes.

Before she could grasp the clothes, he picked up her garments and held them up.

Holding her pajamas just out of her reach, his fingers rubbed the soft flannel. "Things have changed so much." His eyes lowered as he studied the clothing briefly.

"I bet," Gwen said, not daring to move any closer. He had the longest lashes, she couldn't help but notice.

When he looked back up at her, she couldn't stop the intake of breath, her stomach doing the stupid teen-girl flip-flop. Did he know what an enticing picture he made, lying back on her pillows, his clothing straining over the muscular perfection of his body?

As if reading her thoughts, his lips curved.

"It is tempting to forget I am a man of honor. I almost went in there." He motioned to the bathroom with his head. "I 'ave never used an indoor waterfall to bathe under."

"It's called a shower," she said, her voice barely audible, her heartbeat quickening, as she couldn't help but picture him wet and naked. *Don't go there*. She shook her head to clear her muddled mind.

Gwen cleared her throat. "I'll just take my pajamas and then we can talk. We have much to discuss." She inched just a bit closer to the bed reaching for her nightclothes. That was when she noticed the red stain on his shirt. He was bleeding.

"Oh my god!"

Gwen tucked the corner of the towel securing it in place and pulled his shirt open and to the wound on his shoulder. Though the injury seemed to be healing, the flesh around it healthy and pink, a trickle of blood seeped through the jagged cut, down to his chest.

"What happened?"

"Nothing of importance." His warm breath on side of her neck made her realize she was much too close to him. The heat of his skin under her fingertips stalled her momentarily, before she snatched her hand back.

It took tremendous control to meet his gaze. "It's not *nothing*. You're injured and bleeding. It looks like a serious injury." She couldn't help but let her eyes wander across his chest. A feathering of light brown hair covered his pecs, beckoning her to run her fingers over them. "What happened?"

He didn't answer the question, seeming to be distracted by his curiosity. "What is this cloth called?" He held the bottom of her towel, rubbing it between his fingers. It came dangerously close to revealing her butt to the man. She gently pulled the towel out of his grasp.

"It's called terry cloth." Snatching her pajamas out of his other hand, she hurried into the bathroom to change. "Don't go anywhere," she called over her shoulder.

"I couldn't even if I wanted to," Tristan muttered under his breath. He was burning up, a combination of fever and seeing a beautiful woman so scantily covered.

Gwyneth stood taller than the women he was accustomed to, almost reaching his shoulders in height, her body, tantalizing and slender. Fortunately he'd had the opportunity to study her shapely legs, as they were left exposed by the 'terry cloth.'

From the lack of coverage, he could also tell her breasts were plump and full. He couldn't wait to touch them, to cradle them in his palms and suckle their peaks. He adjusted his breeches to allow for the hardness of his want.

"Patience, McRainey," he murmured, looking down at his hardening member. It twitched, getting harder when she came back out, and he almost groaned. Definitely not a good combination, being in pain and aroused.

The enchantress eyed his shoulder, but made no move to

come closer. Instead she sat at the end of the bed, her legs crossed.

Her midnight tresses fell forward as she leaned over and picked up a book and pen. At once she began scribbling notes, her gaze flicking between the book and him.

"I must take advantage of your presence to ask questions so that I can help you. What year were you enchanted?" she began questioning him without preamble.

"It was 1625."

"I was told you were given three days to get your affairs in order, before being cast into the alter-world. What did you do? What terms were you given to break the enchantment?"

Tristan treaded carefully. He had to give her enough information to help her find the right spell to free him, but not let her to be aware of his plan to seduce her.

"To prepare, I did what most men would. I got drunk and slept with as many women as I could." He gave her a lopsided smile.

When she stopped mid-stroke and raised her eyebrows, he shrugged, the action costing him a stab of pain in his shoulder.

"With help from my advisors, I wrote my will, insuring as much as I possibly could that the McRainey lands remained in my family. I hired wizards and enchantresses to try and break the enchantment. Some collected quite handsomely, assuring me they were successful."

He took a breath, his gaze met hers, and he felt a strong pull toward her. As if reading his thoughts, her eyes widened slightly, and she looked back down at her notes.

He continued. "I was told by a wizard who came to help

that the enchantment could only be broken by an enchantress. This part was true, as it was repeated later to us by Meliot himself. That we'd know it was she, because she would be the one who unlocks our ability to move between the two worlds for longer periods and open the lines of communication with the outside world for each of us. He said each enchantress would speak the spell that would finally free us."

"Us?" She gave him a quizzical look. "Who is there with you?"

"Four others, but that is not important at this moment."

Her brow furrowed for a moment and then she turned back to her notes. "So the right spell, by the right enchantress, is what will free you?" Her large brown eyes met his, her thoughts unreadable.

"Aye, and there's a matter of a sacrifice."

"What type of sacrifice?" Her eyes met his, once again a furrowing of her brow and lips pursed.

"That portion will become apparent later." He avoided looking at her and lowered his lashes studying the bedcovers. Then as slowly as possible, he raised his gaze to her. Hearing her intake of breath, he was sure she was not immune to him. Interesting that, after almost four hundred years, his little trick still worked on a female.

"You know my name. How?"

"I overheard it," he replied, not entirely being truthful. He'd been able to pull it from her mind, with his limited mind-reading ability.

"What is the enchanted world like?" she asked, her eyes traveling to the gap in his shirt.

"It's not unlike this one, only more akin to back in my time. There is land and hills, rivers and beasts. The sky is more of a purple hue than blue. Instead of one sun, there are two, sometimes three, and also two moons. The weather in the alter-world varies from mild to very hot. There are no flowers, and most vegetation is green."

He slowed down, watching her write for a couple of beats before continuing. "We are constantly challenged to battle. There are creatures there that do not exist here, like centaurs and dragons."

Her attention rapt, she'd stopped writing. "It sounds very dangerous—we must get you out of there at once."

He started to sit up to reach for her hand, but winced and closed his eyes as a stab of pain knocked him back.

Gwyneth instantly hovered over him. "Are you sure you're alright? Can I get you something?" Her concerned expression made him feel lighter than he'd felt in ages. To have someone care for him was such an alien feeling, after so many years.

"I'll live," he replied. When she touched his forehead with her palm, he winced again. His reaction was not from being in pain, but a woman's touch was almost too much to bear after so long.

"Oh my goodness," Gwyneth cried. "You're burning up. I'll get a cool cloth." She ran into the bathroom.

When she came back with a cold cloth and pressed it to his brow, he sighed. He did not feel well at all, and the distraction of his fever kept him from being able to respond to the pull to return to the alter-world. The tug came again, and he met Gwyneth's gaze. "I should go."

"Can you do it in your current condition?"

He bristled. "Of course."

She watched him for a few beats, her bottom lip trapped by small white teeth. "I don't know. You don't look too good."

He huffed indignantly.

The coolness of the cloth was soothing; without meaning to, he allowed his heavy eyelids to close.

Chapter Eight

Derrick stood outside Gwen's bedroom door. He was about to knock when he heard his aunt's footsteps on the stairwell, and he darted back to his room.

Blasted woman.

He'd planned to ask Gwen to share a glass of wine, feigning insomnia. He wanted to spend more time alone with her. The woman was striking, and if he read things right, interested in him. Her cool attempts to keep him at arm's length only challenged him more.

There was no doubt he'd sleep with her before she left Scotland.

Besides, the closer he got to her, the easier it would be to thwart any plans to remove the McRainey ghost. He needed Tristan McRainey to remain exactly where he was. For years, he'd toiled over every detail of the new McRainey resort, until every aspect of the plan fell perfectly in place.

It had been a painstaking process, having to fight not

only his aunt, but also the town's Council, who all foolishly believed the late Lord McRainey's wishes needed to be adhered to, or bad fortune would befall the entire community.

Damned Scottish and their strong, superstitious nature.

Momentarily, he considered pushing the intercom button, knowing Hannah would answer. The maid would be in his bed without him having to put much effort into seducing her.

However, just the thought of it bored him at the moment.

He went to the large walnut desk at the foot of the bed. On it, the plans for the improved estate were laid out. He ran his fingers over the paper, knowing each detail by heart.

Still, even though he'd memorized every detail, it felt good to see it.

Soon he'd own the most magnificent resort in Scotland, he'd be able to host the elite people of Europe. He'd become a very rich man.

Power charged him, excited him like nothing else could. His lips curved up and he closed his eyes, his hand sliding to his erection.

Thoughts of success always aroused him. He considered taking care of himself. But why do it when there was a willing woman who would be happy to?

He reached to the intercom and pushed the button.

Tristan woke with a start. He'd fallen asleep, and still lay in Gwyneth's bed. Gaining his bearings, he looked to the foot of the bed where she'd sat the night before, at once treated to a beautiful sight.

The enchantress lay across the bed, the notebook by her outstretched hand. She must have taken notes while he slept. How long had he slept? No doubt it was past time for him to return.

He removed the now almost dry cloth from his brow and moved slowly to avoid waking her as he slid off the bed. Pulling the blankets across the bed, he covered her with them. She snuggled into the warmth, her lips curving into a sweet smile. His hand hovered over her face, but he dared not touch her.

He had to leave, the pull from the alter-world almost unbearably strong now. Pulling his shirt back, he studied the wound. The pain of his return leap would not be unbearable now that his wound was almost healed.

He picked up the book and looked at her writing. Several pages contained a full description of him, his clothing and sword, even his mannerisms. She was very thorough. The next words caught his attention. She'd started working on the spell.

Vanquish the shields of time
Remove the walls of deception
Arise the winds of change and move
Unleash the spell of old from its holder
So it is spoken, so let it be done

Tristan read over the words several times, nothing happened, no shift, no sense of any effect. He whispered them again and still nothing. Then a slight shift. Hope swelled. Perhaps the pull affected it. He wondered if they had to chant it together. He peered back down at the sleeping woman and considered waking her. They could try the spell.

Before he could reach out to her, the pull claimed him.

He leaped through the now familiar dark tunnel.

Chapter Nine

Tristan looked across the clearing at Gavin Campbell. The Scot's nod barely perceptible, letting him know the target had moved into place. Tristan tested the line in his hand and waited for Campbell's hand signal.

At the gesture, he yanked on the snare, smiling in grim satisfaction at the large hog they'd caught. The pig's squeals echoed into the forest, so they hurried knowing it would be a matter of minutes before Meliot's scouts were upon them. In one swift motion, Gavin stilled the pig, slicing its throat open, silencing the animal.

Tristan released the snare, allowing the animal to land with a thud. Once the pig was tied, they slid a thin log through its feet and lifted it. Each with an end of the log on his shoulder the men raced back to the keep.

Putting their life in danger for a meal was very reckless, but were it not for taking risks, they'd all be bored to death.

Besides, hunting helped keep their skills honed and movements sharp.

The unmistakable whistle of an approaching arrow caused them to run in a zigzag pattern.

Padraig's shield spell surrounded them, so they weren't too concerned, but why press their luck? Using his extra strength, Tristan grabbed the pig from Gavin, giving the Scot freedom of movement to draw his sword. They raced toward the keep, rounding a gigantic tree only to have their path blocked by three horsemen.

With a war cry, the horsemen attacked.

Tristan dropped the pig, pulled his sword, and rushed forward towards the first rider that reached him. The horseman's sword clashed with his, the horse's side knocking Tristan down.

He rolled and leaped away just as another swing of his opponent's sword descended. He blocked it with ease and dared a glance to Gavin. The Scot held his own, against the other horseman. The one remaining horseman stayed back, surveying the scene.

It was as if the horseman's body was made of air because when Tristan's sword slashed across his mid-section, slicing the creature in two, there was no scream nor blood.

An instant later, the horseman vanished, and Gavin's opponent vanished as well. Both of them held their swords in front of them, turning to face off against the solitary man, who remained atop his horse.

Silently, his black gaze followed their movements, then he held his hands up as a sign that he was not a threat. Nonetheless, they did not relax their stance. The man dismounted and stood before them still not speaking. Then he removed his helmet.

There was no mistaking who stood before them. Meliot's soulless eyes flashed over them, and they braced for a bolt of whatever energy he was about to fire at them.

Instead, the wizard pursed his lips giving them a lazy look.

He looked to the carcass and shook his head. "Why do you hunt? You have no need for nourishment. A gift from me."

When they did not reply, he shrugged. "No gratitude required. Time for another challenge gentlemen," he told them stepping away from his horse.

The wizard stood, a tall, gray-haired man with strong sharp features. His nose was long, his cheeks prominent. He wore a beard, but it was always trimmed so one could note the slender jawline. Other than his hair, not much changed in his appearance over the years, his face remained unlined, and his posture erect. He looked every bit the seventeenth-century wizard, except for his way of dress. Meliot did not wear robes, but a tunic and hose like them.

With his hands behind his back, the man paced.

Tristan and Gavin remained on alert even though Meliot did not need a sword to fling them into another place or situation.

"What is it this time, Wizard?" Tristan asked, keeping his sights on the wizard's hands.

Gavin didn't give him time to speak. "Must be an exceptional challenge that you would deliver the missive in person."

Meliot's lips curved, addressing Gavin with a wave of his hand. "Not necessarily."

He lifted his hands; Tristan and Gavin braced and then charged forward. Meliot and his horse vanished, only the sound of his voice remaining.

"Enjoy," a voice called out, as they were flung into darkness.

THEY LANDED in a clearing in the forest. Before they could gather their bearings, Padraig, Liam and Niall, appeared at the same time.

A horse for each of them stood nearby.

"We must go and fast," Liam warned.

Immediately the five men mounted and barely took a moment to grab the reins before taking off at full speed.

The thunder of the horses' hooves that gave chase echoed Tristan's heartbeats as they raced through the dense woods.

He turned to look. About twenty warriors chased them. Horsemen wearing helmets so he could not discern who they were. Not that it mattered; most of the time, the beings in that world were fabricated by Meliot.

Coming to a fork in the path, Liam motioned that they should take different paths, and they split off. During times like these, they communicated with hand signals to keep whoever challenged as unaware of their plans as possible.

Niall, Padraig and Liam went in the opposite direction from the one Tristan and Gavin took. Tristan's power of extraordinary strength made up for an extra man, so they were evenly divided.

As expected, their pursuers split evenly behind them.

Gavin whistled and gave a quick hand signal telling him to prepare for attack. Once they reached a clearing, they stopped and turned to face the riders coming at them.

Before lowering the face guard of his helmet, Tristan met Gavin's amused gaze, the man actually enjoying the prospect of the fight. Gavin Campbell lived for two things, battle and tournaments. Being that tournaments were non-existent in the alter-world, he was primed for the impending contest. Letting out a blood curdling battle cry, the huge Scot charged toward their enemies. Tristan almost laughed, noting that the enemy actually faltered at the sight.

The sound of swords clashing, grunts, and horses' whinnying filled the air, echoed from the trees. Not able to take the time to keep an eye on Gavin while defending himself, Tristan hoped for the best and blocked a sword's decent meant to cut him down.

As often with Meliot's challenges, there were clues in every obstacle. This meant that perhaps one of the horsemen had a clue to winning this challenge. They could not kill any of them until they could figure out which one. It proved a hard task. Incapacitating them meant they could rise and strike again.

His current opponent's soulless black eyes didn't register pain when Tristan relieved him of his sword arm. Instead, he picked up his sword with the other hand to strike at him again.

They continued, fighting, maiming only for their soulless opponents to rise and attack again. Sweat flowed down his brow making it hard to see. Not able to resist, Tristan swung wide slicing across two opponents' midsections. They crumpled to the ground and remained there.

Jumping back to avoid a hammer's blow to his own midsection, Tristan stabbed behind him and heard a grunt. He'd hit his mark. With a groan, the male fell from his horse. A hammer-wielding warrior crooked his head to the side, studying him. That's when he noticed the red dragon emblem on the right shoulder.

The clue.

He ventured a glance toward Gavin, and gave two quick whistles, letting Gavin know he'd found the clue. That was all the Scot needed. Within moments four bodies lay at his feet.

Tristan circled, not quite sure how to handle the dragon warrior. He didn't want to kill him, in case the clue was a verbal one, yet it wasn't like he would come with them voluntarily. The decision was taken away from him when the giant crumpled to his knees and then face forward into the dirt. Gavin gave him a shrug when Tristan glared at him.

"He's not dead. Just out for a bit," Gavin explained, then seeing one of the downed moved, he drove his sword into the offender's chest. "Stay dead," Gavin commanded the body.

Gavin Campbell was a total and complete contradiction in terms. The beauty of the man a stark contrast to the bloodthirsty warrior he became in battle.

Back when they lived a normal existence, Campbell was perpetually annoyed. Each time he entered any room or approached people, his ravishing good looks caused both men and women to take pause and notice.

One almost felt sorry for him, although it was hard to.

Campbell, a large man, a head over six feet, with an expansive muscular chest and bulging arms, wore his blond hair long, just to his shoulders, and constantly sported a beard-shadowed jaw line. His heavily lashed amber eyes were large, his nose straight. The man's looks were impossible to describe. It could only be said that, in Gavin's case, seeing definitely was believing.

Tristan did not envy Campbell his attractiveness—all the attention had made it hard for the man to move unnoticed.

And yet, he wasn't perfect. His one flaw: outside the battlefield, Gavin was clumsy as an ox.

When his childhood friend first approached Tristan, offering his sword to his service, Tristan was dubious as to why a leader of one of Scotland's most powerful clans would do such a thing. The Scot offered no explanation other than stating he'd left his clan in the hands of a capable younger brother until his return.

Many speculated that The Campbell was a warrior, and could never be content to remain behind while his fellow clansmen fought. The Campbell clan, one of the strongest, rarely needed to defend its lands from other clan attacks. Tristan suspected the reason for Campbell leaving his clan was more of a personal one.

Now he was thankful for it, because through the years of their enchantment, after knowing each other for so long, they were suited to hunting and warring together.

Just as Tristan and Gavin finished securing their "clue," the other knights arrived. They dismounted and came over to study the prisoner.

"Any idea what we're looking to get from him?" Liam

asked, his foot tapping the dragon emblem on the man's shoulder. "He say anything?"

"No more than grunts so far," Tristan replied. "Perhaps we need to figure out what the red dragon signifies."

They studied it. A red dragon crouched, his front paw curled around a lightning bolt. His tail circled a sphere, on the sphere the emblem of a lion. The same lion as the one on the amulet Tristan wore.

Suddenly Liam held both hands out for silence and his eyes shut. "The mountain of lightning houses a dragon."

Then he opened his eyes and looked at them, shrugging. "Whatever that means, I am not sure. I say we are to go forth and convince him to share his toys with us." Liam motioned toward snowcapped mountains to their right.

A disgusted look on his face, Gavin pulled out his dirk and cut the dragon emblem from the prisoner's breastplate, while the downed man didn't stir but watched through cold, flat eyes.

He held the emblem up studying it. "Is this a foresight, Murray? Or are ye just making up shit?"

Liam's jaw visibly tensed, but he didn't reply. Instead, he turned away and looked up at the cloudless sky and raised his arms, palms up, as he often did when seeking foresight. A grunt from their prisoner the only sound as they waited.

Tristan kneeled down to the warrior and pulled his helmet off. Other than cloudy eyes, the soulless creature didn't project any emotion. "What is your purpose?" Tristan asked him.

No answer.

"Tell me why I shouldn't end your miserable life right now."

The creature seemed to consider his answer before speaking. "I know where the dragon's lair is." The voice a mixture of many.

"So do I." Tristan pulled out his dirk, about to cut the cursed thing's throat, when Liam's curt order stopped him.

"He must accompany us. The reason will become clear."

Chapter Ten

Gwen didn't know what to think when she woke up on the edge of the bed covered with the spare blanket. If it wasn't for the damp cloth Tristan left on the side table, she'd convince herself it'd been another strange dream. Maybe this was it. She'd finally gone over the edge like her Great-Aunt Bernice.

Aunt Bernice, her grandmother's sister, had spent the last years of her life in a mental institution, convinced the ghost of a Civil War general followed her around like a puppy. Her aunt would insist people acknowledge the general, to the point of becoming angry if one looked in the wrong direction when talking to him.

Gwen wondered if they'd been unfair to Aunt Bernice. After the past few days, she could sincerely relate.

Would she come to the same belief as Edith? That Tristan McRainey was a real man, not a ghost, a man trapped in an enchantment. An enchantment, which could only be broken by her.

Reaching for her cell phone, she called her sisters. Faced with the tremendous situation, she needed their help.

She also needed for them to pull out their most precious item when faced with situations like this. It was a book of spells their mother had used when training them.

The "Magic book," as they'd come to call it, contained recipes for potions, the aged pages filled with scribbles and notes from generations past. There were spells, letters, and all kinds of annotations referring to certain experiences. Everything was covered, from simple elixirs for aches, to dealing with the paranormal.

Gwen and her sisters currently shared a spacious condo in the Buckhead area of Atlanta. Originally, Gwen had purchased it. Her sister Sabrina, a photographer, had moved in a year later, upon accepting a photo shoot that would last months.

Although Sabrina considered Atlanta her residence, the successful photographer spent most of her time traveling all over the world for shoots.

The youngest, Tamara, had recently moved into the condo after a breakup. The consummate free spirit and fun company to have, Gwen doubted Tamara would remain long.

When Tamara's voice chirped a *hello*, Gwen couldn't help but smile, picturing the pixie sitting cross-legged on the bed, probably in pink shorts and t-shirt, her blonde hair in a messy ponytail.

"Hey, Sis," Tammie exclaimed. "I'm so glad you called. Sabrina and I were wondering how it's been going." She continued without giving Gwen a chance to answer—typical.

"How beautiful is that place? It looks amazing from the pictures you sent."

Sabrina must have taken the phone from Tammie. "Hey, Sis. Please tell me there is a handsome laird who lives in that castle. I am tempted to rush there just to take pictures."

"There is one man who will inherit the castle. His name is Derrick and yes, he is handsome," Gwen said, wanting to tell them about Tristan and how she found him much more alluring.

She had to move the phone away from her ear at Tammie's excited scream. "I am googling him right now."

Ignoring her sister, Gwen continued. "I am faced with something a bit different than I expected. The woman who hired me insists the apparition is not a ghost, but someone trapped in an enchantment of some sort. I am definitely going to need to refer to the Magic Book."

Sabrina's husky voice sounded serious. "You need the book? Really? How are we going to get it to you? We can't very well mail it."

Gwen fidgeted a little. She hadn't thought about that. "Video call?"

"Or, how about you give me more specifics and we research it for you. Tammie and I can work on the spell from here?" Sabrina said.

"Okay." Gwen blew out a breath. "I am not sure how to begin, but the gist is that four men, they called themselves knights, are trapped in an enchantment by a wizard. Each has a different set of circumstances, and each needs a specific person with special powers to free them."

She went on to tell them about the interactions with

Tristan, while referring to her notes. "He touched me, and his fingers were warm," Gwen told them.

"Whoa," Sabrina said, after a beat of silence. "Sounds like a complicated job. We've never dealt with something like this. If it's even real."

Tamara soundless breathless with excitement. "Do you think the woman who hired you made all of it up? I mean, I do believe you about the ghost, but the rest seems far-fetched."

"Maybe I'm in over my head," Gwen admitted. "I may not be equipped for this. Perhaps I should leave before making things worse."

Sabrina huffed. "Of course you're not... don't be silly. You of all people are more than well-suited to figure this out." Gwen could hear paper rustling, and Sabrina's breathing for a few moments.

"Are you looking in the book now?"

"Yes. Wait, I'm looking, enchantments, knights, wizard..."

After a few minutes of spouting words that didn't connect, Sabrina finally spoke to her again. "Okay, nothing. We won't be able to do much until you get us more info."

Gwen slumped. "What more should I find out?"

"You need to find out the circumstances leading up the enchantment. You said they were on their way to meet with a group of knights. Was it their plan to pledge their swords to their cause? Why did the wizard take offense at whatever they did or were planning to do? If you can give me that reason, the root of the conflict between the knights and this wizard, it will be easier for us to figure out which spell and wards will help break the enchantment."

It didn't feel like the odds were in their favor.

"I will call you once I speak to him again. Hopefully I can get all the information we need. He disappears quickly at times."

After they disconnected, Gwen grabbed her journal and began to write down all the information she needed to gather from Tristan.

Now all she had to do was wait for him to reappear.

Chapter Eleven

Steam rose from their horses and the men's shoulders, as they climbed the steep, curving road that led to the opening on the side of the mountain. Interesting, to be sweating while sloshing through almost knee-high snow. But the suns on their backs blazed as strongly as a hot summer day. Tristan, like the other men, walked in front of his horse, the animal's reins in his hand as he tested each step he took, careful not to step too wide and slip into the deep ravine below. Padraig urged his horse along magically as he held the reins of the horse that carried their prisoner.

A rumble vibrated the ground under their feet, and they stilled, waiting, while at the same time scanning the sky for any sign of the dragon. Even the horses seemed to sense the threat and became uncharacteristically quiet.

Giving a signal, Liam urged them forward. His gift of foresight, although invaluable in times like these, did not stop them from being overly cautious. Together they'd come to this damned place and together they'd leave. The men had vowed that not one of them would ever be left behind.

Finally arriving at a wider opening at the side of the mountain, one by one, they led their steeds to the clearing and mounted.

They rode at a steady pace until they reached a brook. Then waited, hidden in the trees as Liam scanned the area a few paces in front of them.

"He's here," the prisoner grunted, then without another word, he fell forward off his mount and vanished.

A dragon's screech is something a man could never forget. The sound echoed into the trees, followed by the flapping of its gigantic wings as the beast glided into view. The body of the dragon a dark green hue, with scales that shimmered into violets and blues where the sun's rays touched. Talons extended, it descended towards them, letting out another screech before cutting past them, flying so close the wind from its wings caused their heads to snap back. The men clutched on to the horses' reins, to keep from falling off their mounts.

They retreated into the woods, although considering the size of the beast, no tree could stop it if it decided to come after them.

Tristan held his hand up and they stopped. "Our best chance to beat him is by getting the thing to land. I say we get it to follow us to the clearing up ahead. It will have to land to attack."

He locked gazes with Liam. "What say you?"

Liam shook his head. "Something is not right. The dragon could have attacked us while we climbed, yet it waited for us to arrive at the brook to make its presence known. Again, he didn't attack. I agree that if we are to vanquish it, we must get it to stand on solid ground."

Hoping to bait the dragon, they burst from the trees as one, the horses galloping at a high speed. Tristan didn't have to look over his shoulder to know the dragon was close behind, the combination of its low growls and the whooshing sound of its wings alerted him to its nearness.

As they neared a clearing, they brought the horses to a stop and Padraig released the riderless horse. Communicating with hand signals, they surrounded the open space from inside the tree line.

The dragon would have lost sight of the group and could only keep moving forward until the clearing. Just as they hoped, it dove straight toward the terrified horse, who barely managed to escape. The beast landed, its huge head swinging side to side before releasing a loud screech.

The knights burst into the clearing, faces taut with the anticipation of the fight. Swords were drawn, held high. The dragon reared up on its hind legs, towering over the riders, its red eyes focused, its nostrils flared. As its foot-long talons sliced the air in front of Tristan's horse, he flung his sword into the air aiming for the beast's heart.

The blade sank into the creature's chest, followed by the swords of the other knights. Each weapon drove into the dragon's flesh with a sickening thud. The beast screeched, falling backward, landing on its side and toppling trees with its enormous weight. The dragon's tail lashed about, causing Gavin's horse to fall over, throwing the knight. Tristan and the others jumped off their mounts, their spare swords in hand as they charged towards the downed beast.

Everything was much too easy. The fact their swords had sunk into the beast was hard to believe.

Hollow laughter filled the air as the dragon raised its head, and the glowing eyes met Tristan's. It suddenly became clear who the dragon was. It was Meliot. It had all been some sort of illusion.

The dragon shuddered and stilled, as if dead. No one moved, waiting to see if something else would happen. Just then a small sphere rolled into the clearing. Tristan stepped forward and looked down at it. It was the size of an egg, clear like glass with a red lion suspended in the center.

Gavin came up beside him. Placing his hand on Tristan's shoulder he studied the sphere. "Well done, McRainey."

"Then why do I feel like this was a big fucking waste of time," Tristan replied, picking up the sphere.

Before Gavin could answer him, they were transported back to their keep. In the great room, a meal of roasted pig greeted them.

Chapter Twelve

It was the second day without even a glimpse of Tristan McRainey. If he didn't appear soon, she would have to tell Edith her job here was done. As much as she wanted to help Edith keep the McRainey estate private, the more she thought about it, the more she believed Tristan had just been a ghost, a strong apparition. She'd been caught up in the experience and overreacted, but in the end, there was no enchantment.

Gwen stared out the window at the approaching car. Derrick arrived to take her horseback riding. Yesterday, he'd come for her and treated her to lunch in town. She knew the man was interested in her, and she should probably put a stop to it, but she was beginning to like the guy.

There were qualities about him that she couldn't deny finding attractive. Derrick was attentive and handsome, not to mention the Scottish accent. Every time he talked, her insides melted.

Besides, what harm could come of it? She'd be leaving

soon. Smoothing her short coat, she picked up her gloves and headed outside.

He looked every bit Lord of the Manor in his blue riding jacket, tan breeches, and black boots. Derrick's eyes were quick to assess her fully before meeting her gaze. He leaned forward, kissing her cheek in greeting. Every inch the gentleman, he took her elbow and guided her to the stables.

"I trust you slept well, Gwen," he stated, her first name somehow sounding richer.

"Yes, I did actually," she replied, smiling up at him.

"Anything new?" he asked nonchalantly.

She knew he referred to Tristan and answered truthfully. "No, not at all. Strange that he appeared so often and then suddenly nothing. I am going to have to tell your aunt there's nothing more I can do."

Derrick studied her. "You seem disappointed."

"I am. If your ancestor's ghost is trapped here, it's sad. I feel it's best to allow the dead to move on."

She met his dubious look. "Look, I know you have plans for this place, but whether it remains a private home or not, it's always good for the deceased to find peace." A dull ache tightened her chest, and she stop speaking. It was obvious Derrick had no interest in what she did for a living and was dubious about anything relating to his dead ancestor.

The conversation turned to casual topics about the horses as they walked the rest of the way to the stables. A man, whom Derrick introduced as Miles O'Reilly, walked out with their respective mounts and waited patiently until they neared.

Derrick assisted her to mount, giving her short instructions, claiming the horse was tame and needed little guidance. It turned out to be true. Her mare was gentle, making it easy for her, as she was a novice rider.

On a larger horse, Derrick rode alongside, his attention on her and the horse until he seemed to consider she was at ease.

"If at any time you feel uncomfortable, let me know. Horses can sense our emotions and be affected," he informed her.

After a few moments they arrived at the water's edge, the creek's clear water bubbling past adding to the picturesque scene. Derrick dismounted and came to help her down. Holding the horses' reins, they allowed the animals to drink.

Something about Derrick's penetrating gaze was unsettling. He seemed a bit too intense today, at times making Gwen a bit uneasy. Perhaps some people found deep stares alluring, but it was a bit much, especially the way he stared at her at times without blinking.

She made small talk, hoping to calm her apprehension. "It's so beautiful here, I won't ever forget it."

"I'd be disappointed if you left before I'd have the opportunity to kiss you." He moved closer, his intent clear.

Gwen wasn't sure if she wanted to kiss him. Admittedly, she found him attractive, and it would be fun, but at the same time, there was something that didn't feel right.

Taking her by the shoulders, he leaned forward, his lips barely touching hers. Gwen was about to push away when a clap of thunder caused them both to jump.

At the second boom from the skies, the horses took off at a gallop heading for the stables, leaving them stranded.

Dark clouds began rolling in and Gwen stifled an amused hysterical outburst of laughter at nature helping to make the kiss less awkward. "I think we should make a run for it. It looks like a mean storm."

They'd barely begun the trek back to the house when Miles appeared driving a golf cart.

He pointed back toward the stables. "I was near when the horses raced past," he explained, his gaze moving over them. "Was either of you hurt?"

Both shook their heads and climbed onto the golf cart.

THE GOLF CART'S cover was no match for the rain, and by the time Gwen made her way inside and to her bedroom, she was drenched.

"So much for a day of riding," she grumbled, peeling off her coat and letting it drip from a hanger in the bathroom.

Derrick had gone home, promising to return for dinner after he'd changed. For some reason Gwen felt ill at ease about the kiss they'd exchanged. It was silly of course, they were both single, there was nothing more to it than flirtation on his part. Then there was the fact he was handsome, titled, and rich. What else could a girl want?

He wasn't Tristan.

In her bathroom, after she peeled the rest of the soaked clothing, she dried off with a large fluffy towel, letting the water run until it warmed. Once the stream of water grew hot, she washed off her ruined make-up and blotted her face dry. When she looked back up into the mirror, she a startled yelp escaped.

Tristan McRainey stood right behind her.

She swung around to face him and admonish him for scaring her, but before she could utter a word, his mouth took hers in a savage kiss.

The way he held her, his lips claimed hers, confirmed, beyond a doubt, Tristan was no ghost.

His hard body against hers, warm lips covering hers and tongue circling with hers, all real. *Oh yes, very real.*

His body was warm and solid, thick and muscular. He smelled of moss and pine and tasted like spice and wine. Every single one of her senses were filled to overflowing. The towel fell, the only reason she realized it was the warmth of his hands on her bare skin, when he cupped her bottom, lifting her intimately against him.

No man could evoke such a response from her with but a kiss. There was no reason for it, no sense to it, but in that moment, Gwen knew she had to be with him. She needed to claim him and make him hers.

"Make love to me, Tristan."

HER WORDS CUT through the fog of his anger and want. When he'd seen her kissing the young McRainey, he'd lost his temper which seemed to have caused the storm. He was tipping to the point of no return.

The enchantress had to fall in love with him, it was the only way for him to escape, but at the same time, he wanted her to for other unexplainable reasons.

Her breath came in short pants, her lips nibbled deliciously on his neck as she ran her fingers through his hair. No doubt she desired him. Would behaving like a cad help or hurt his chance at claiming her heart?

Gwyneth began to pull at his clothing and succeeding in removing his tunic. When they separated just enough for her to pull it over his head and their gazes met, he drowned in the dark pools. Desire took control. He finished undressing while she touched and titillated him, until his entire body vibrated with want.

They clashed again. He no longer pondered the outcome, her velvety soft flesh all-consuming under his lips, his hands. When they reached her bed, they fell into it, not breaking their kiss.

The alluring woman lay atop him without inhibitions, the most alluring thing ever. Those fingers marked a wonderful trail down his chest, her tongue followed closely behind, circling and nipping. Her delicious mouth made him unable to do more than moan and grunt, straining not to come before even entering her.

Her torture continued as she slid down his body toward his mid-section, leaving his flesh quivering in anticipation. When she began to flick her tongue around the engorged head of his cock, his hips thrust forward of their own accord, and he fisted the bed covering, fighting again not to finish.

Acknowledging that he could not take much more, she moved back over him. He immediately took advantage, rolling her over, their bodies pressed together. While he feasted on her lips, her hands to travel down his back cupping his buttocks. So much he wanted to do, prolong the moment forever.

She gasped when he took her nipple into his mouth, suckling, enjoying her movements under him.

"You're amazing," she gasped. "I can't get enough of you."

Tristan liked her boldness, and he smiled at her. "I must have you now."

Not looking away from his face, she reached between them and took him in hand. "Then take me."

Sinking into her, they both let out a loud sigh of relief. The joining of their bodies was like nothing he'd experienced. He lost control completely and allowed his body to take over, moving in and out of her in the fast rhythm of need and urgency that overrode any thought or command.

She screamed his name and began to move with him. Meeting him thrust for thrust, as if she too felt the urgent need for them to come together.

On and on, the pace continued until sweat dripped from him, and still he could not slow. As a wave of ecstasy crested, another swelled and they both clung to each other, the sounds of her moans echoing in his ears.

Finally, he peaked, sensations slamming so hard he moaned deep in his throat as his release made him shudder. Her sex constricted around him, milking him for all he could give, as she crested yet again.

Chapter Thirteen

Mind-blowing sex just happened.

She'd heard the term used many a time, but now, this very day, she could confirm that it really existed. And furthermore, she could confirm that if Tristan McRainey was indeed a ghost, he had to be the heaviest one ever. He sprawled over her where he'd collapsed after coming for what seemed like the third time.

His weight didn't bother her, actually she found it comforting. Gwen swept his hair away from the side of his face and kissed him just below his jaw line. He barely budged, his only response a soft grunt.

She'd had a one-night stand once, with a guy she'd picked up at a hotel bar, but for the most part, she was a get-to-know-them-first kind of girl. And sleeping with someone connected to her job... well, she'd never done that.

This was a first on so many levels. Tristan was job-related, an older man. Way older. And he was also supposed to be a ghost. Not to mention that she had plans with his great-great-great-who-knows-how-many-greats-nephew that evening.

Gwen closed her eyes, running her hands down his broad back. The man's body was totally amazing.

"Oh God," she groaned, hugging Tristan to her. He felt too good to let go. "What are you?"

Tristan rolled off to the side taking her with him, since she refused to release him. She wiggled yet closer to him. He tipped her face up to him. "I'm a man. I think I've just proved it to ye, lass."

She would have rolled her eyes at his look of satisfaction, if it weren't for the fact that he not only proved it, but he'd gone way above and beyond the call of proving it.

"Yes, you did," Gwen replied, not sure what else to say. "Tristan, I am not sure why what just happened happened, but I'm here to do a job. My purpose is to find out how to free you. I am positive that having sex with you was not the best idea."

His lips curved into a smile and Gwen bit her lip to keep from kissing him. So unfair for him to be so tempting. She had to get her head out of the clouds and help him. Otherwise, he'd be trapped forever.

Thoughtful, he lowered his gaze and pressed his lips together. "I hope I have not offended ye by this, Gwyneth. It was not my intention, to be with ye. At least not right away. I will not deny, I wanted ye from the first moment I saw ye."

She immediately felt bad for making the comments. After all, she was the one who'd initiated things. "No, of course not. Tristan, I don't regret any part of what just happened. It was amazing. It was beautiful, being with you. It's just that, what is most important is freeing you, and we're wasting valuable time."

Nodding, he relaxed and smiled. He kissed her again, and instantly calmness engulfed her, like a tidal wave of cool water over a parched desert—she wanted to soak it all in. Somehow she found the strength to pull away.

She got off the bed, grabbed up her discarded sweatpants and tugged them on, then began to yank on a t-shirt. "I'm going to run downstairs to speak to Edith and tell her that I will be working with you for a bit. I'm coming right back." She wanted to cry at the picture that lay before her. Tristan listening intently, his handsome face solemn, completely nude, lying on his side watching her. It took the strength of Samson not to jump back into bed with him.

"And, please for the love of all that's holy, get dressed, or I can promise you, we won't get any work done."

She backed away toward the door. "Don't leave." Then she turned and rushed from the room.

When Gwen got to the first floor, she almost collided with Edith.

"Goodness child, are you alright?" Edith seemed to be taking in her appearance. "You must have gotten caught in the rain. Perhaps you should take a hot shower."

Gwen caught sight of her appearance in the mirror. Her shirt was on inside out, her hair was a tangled mess, and her face flushed.

"Yes, I will. I will take a shower, but I just saw the ghost... er, I mean Tristan McRainey. He's upstairs," She blabbered, pointing to the ceiling. "I am going to get as much information as I can, so please don't be surprised if I don't come down for dinner. Please give my apologies to Derrick." She flew back up the stairs without waiting for a response from Edith, who smiled the entire time she explained.

When Gwen returned to the bedroom, she hesitated before opening the door. She leaned in to listen, but there were no sounds from inside. Hopefully Tristan was dressed and not still lying about, an open temptation to do more than just get information from him.

The sight of him fully dressed looking intently out of the window didn't calm her lust any, the setting sun providing just enough light to give him a staged setting. He looked down towards the courtyard, brow furrowed, seeming to be in deep thought. His gaze flickered to her, and he nodded in acknowledgement but didn't speak.

"Why do you always stand at the windows? Can you not go outside?"

"Aye, I have not been able to will myself outside of the house since the enchantment. Through windows I can see quite far." The drawing together of his brow indicated a solemn mood. "By looking through the windows of this house, I can see much of the estate. I have learned a great deal and seen many changes throughout the years.

"It must be so hard." Gwen's heart ached. "I can't imagine being held prisoner for so many years. How have you and the others withstood it?"

He responded with a bitter laugh. "We haven't. Not really. At first, Meliot's fury was fresh, making life chaotic and very hard, one ridiculous challenge after another. At one time or another, each of us has almost reached madness, escaping inward to survive." He moved from the window, tearing his eyes away from the landscape reluctantly. "Over the years, the challenges slowed. We're either attacked or sent on some ridiculous quest perhaps once a year."

"Yet he never kills you?"

"The last night, before we were not to wake in this world again, an enchantress who'd tried to free Liam gave each of us a talisman." He lifted out the leather strap around his neck. From it hung a stamped flat pewter piece.

"Each amulet has a different stamp to signify a power. These strengths have been invaluable."

He shook his head. "Of course I don't believe Meliot will allow us to die. Hurt or torture us, yes, the finality and peace of death, no. He wants to ensure we survive as his prisoners until we can witness his return to complete the thwarted plan. Only then will he allow us to die." His matter-of-fact tone when speaking of his death troubled her.

"Tell me about the others."

Tristan sat and studied her for a long moment, as if evaluating her worth. Gwen imagined it was hard for him to believe that she, an insignificant woman in his eyes, could possibly save him. But his expression did not reveal his thoughts. As he watched her, the only thing reflected in them was a deep longing. He longed to be free and no matter what she had to do, she'd see him free.

"Gavin Campbell is Scottish," he began, smiling when

she scrambled to pick up her notebook. "He is the largest among us, but probably the gentlest. He was laird to the most powerful clan in Scotland, Clan Campbell. Gavin is also very fair to look upon. He calls it a curse, what so many men would give an eye-tooth for. His beauty proved to be the undoing of many a maiden during his time, and the bards sang of it even centuries after we'd gone. He received the power of seduction, again much to his chagrin."

Gwen smiled at the thought of a handsome man hating his effect on women. "Please continue," she urged.

"Niall MacTavish and Padraig Clarre are both fellow Scots. Niall, the Duke of Lennox, lost his wife and children upon being enchanted. Something he will not discuss or tolerate questions about. Niall, a quiet man who prefers his own company, received the power of healing, which has saved us much pain and suffering. Padraig is the opposite of Niall. Padraig, a jokester, has a sunny disposition and seems to see the best in every situation. He is young, was only two-and-twenty when enchanted. With the power of magic, and his immaturity, the lad is lucky to have survived this long." Tristan's smile was fond. He waited until she finished writing to continue.

"Lastly there is Liam. Liam, an Englishman, a noble, was someone we'd not met until that day at the village. The Brit is one of the best swordsmen I have ever encountered, and swift as well. His has the power of foresight, can see the future, but is limited to the immediate for the most part." Tristan became pensive and ran his hand through his hair. "Liam and Gavin are always at odds. They got along well in the very beginning, like the rest of us, just trying to survive and make sense of things. Then one day they must have quarreled over something quite serious, because they've been at each other's throat since."

Gwen flipped the page. "Tell me about the village, about the day you found out you'd be enchanted."

Chapter Fourteen

1625, SCOTLAND

The dust from the horses' hooves gave the road before him a hazy appearance. Tristan pulled his cowl up to cover his face, blinking rapidly. His eyes stung from the combination of dirt and sweat. For days, he and the three of the King James's knights, Niall MacTavish, Padraig Clarre, and Gavin Campbell, kept up the hard pace, stopping only to sleep for a couple of hours, catching what they could to eat, and then riding again.

The instructions were clear, the missive instructing them to present themselves before the council of knights by midday on the last day of the fasting.

Although the founder of the council had been dead for many years, the knight's order remained. He and the three men, after numerous threats from the Norse, were more than ready to pledge their swords and those of their respective clans to join forces against the tyranny of the Vikings. It was imperative that they arrive in time to make their pledge before the hearings ended.

The clouds of smoke were the first signs of something amiss, followed by the sounds of women's screams and children's cries. Tristan pulled his horse to a stop and waited for the others to catch up to him.

"We can't stop," Padraig told them, his usually jovial façade gone. "Those poor people are going to have to fend for themselves."

"And turn our backs on them?" The Campbell, ever the crusader, replied astonished. "I cannot do that."

"Even if we keep our current pace, we are still dangerously close to missing the council before they separate after their last hearing. We have been delayed by obstacle after obstacle and cannot afford to be delayed again." Niall MacTavish's gaze pinned to the Campbell's. "Our clans' lives are at stake."

"What say you McRainey?" Campbell turned his horse to face Tristan. "Do we walk away?"

Just then a woman stumbled into the road, bloody and ashen, she held up her child to them. As MacTavish reached to steady her, she fell dead, an arrow protruding from her back. The child wailed. Without thought, Tristan spurned his horse towards the village, he and Campbell riding as fast as they could urge their horses forward.

When he looked over his shoulder, Niall followed. Padraig was further back; he had dismounted and was securing the child against a tree. The child would be safe until someone came for it.

To say the scene was bloody would be the ultimate

understatement; rivers of red flowed from every hut in the village. Only a handful of men remained, barely able to fight.

Young women were being thrown into cages on carts. They screamed as a few of the surviving males fought the losing battle against huge, chainmail-clad horsemen.

When the four knights burst into the village, there was a momentary stillness as everyone looked to see what occurred.

Catching the horsemen by surprise, Tristan and Gavin were able to cut several of them down. The advantage was soon gone, and by the time Niall and Padraig entered the fray, they were met with strong opposition.

The battle between the knights and the horsemen became brutal. The horsemen fought with no fear, not seeming to care if they were injured. They were like no opponent he'd ever faced.

Tristan, bleeding from a wound to his side, finally felled an opponent only to face another. He slid a glance to check on the others. Gavin who fought two men. The huge Scot seemed to be holding his own, but he had to be tiring. Niall felled his opponent, sinking his sword into the fallen man, as if to insure he stayed down.

After managing to beat the man he fought, Tristan rushed forward to help Gavin. Out of the corner of his eyes, he caught sight of Padraig unlatching the cages, releasing the trapped women.

As they ran for safety, a horsemen attacked them. Tristan was astounded at their lack of humanity when he saw two young maidens fall dead from the horseman's sword. Before he could cut down a third, a blond man on horseback broke into the fray.

The man's sword skills were impressive, his defense not allowing for any strikes as he defended the women, cutting down his opponent and swiftly moved to the next. After a moment, he and Gavin could attempt to catch their breath, as the newcomer dispatched one opponent after another.

The few attackers who could mount fled, not seeming to care that they left their comrades behind.

The aftermath of the fight could only be described as dreamlike. The people of the small village scrambled about, most of them crying and desperately looking for survivors. The injured were carried indoors to be cared for, the dead surrounded by their loved ones.

The knights assisted with moving the injured and setting up makeshift pallets for them to lie upon.

When all that could be done was done, they knew it was too late to arrive in time to be meet with the Knights' Council, who'd surely disbanded by now.

Refusing food and shelter from the already shattered villagers, the men prepared a camp nearby to rest before heading back to their perspective clans.

They invited the newcomer, Liam Murray, to join them. He turned out to be an English knight who also planned to meet with the council.

Although Tristan was glad to have rescued the villagers from a horrible fate, he was disheartened that he'd not accomplished what needed to be done for his clan's people. They too could face death and injury if the Norse continued to move inland in their attacks.

"We should sleep in shifts," Niall informed them. "The attackers were not normal. I do nae doubt they can come back and attack us."

Whilst the other three lay on bedrolls around a fire, Tristan and Padraig took the first shift of guard duty. Grim in the knowledge that they'd return to their clans without good news, they didn't bother with conversation, but instead patrolled the perimeter of their area in silence.

The full moon gave them enough light to see as they walked, the eerie silence of the surroundings almost engulfing them. Suddenly, an unnatural howl filled the air.

Tristan and Padraig rushed into the camp finding the others already on their feet, swords in hand.

The air was still, the surroundings once again plunged into silence as they turned in circles scanning the surroundings. The flames from the fire rose, swaying in the nonexistent breeze. The flames swirled and twisted until taking form. The flames became a torso, arms, a head, and face, all waving in unison, as the creature faced them.

"Ye killed my men. Ye foiled my plans. Ye will pay dearly." The creature, which resembled an old man, lanced fire at them making them jump backward to avoid being burnt.

Holding up his shield, Tristan advanced.

"Ye sent them to kill and trap innocent people."

"Silence." The creature spat blue flames at him, causing him to shift sideways. "The maidens were to become the mothers of my children, the next generation of great power."

The entity had to be bound by a time restraint, else it wouldn't be so angry. Tristan narrowed his eyes. "Return to where ye come from. Ye have no place here."

The creature seemed to laugh because cackles erupted, making Tristan's skin crawl. "I do have some boundaries I can nae cross. That does nay stop me from bringing punishment."

The campfire returned to normal. The sounds of crickets and other night noises returned shortly after.

Not sure if the creature was gone or just giving them a temporary respite, the men remained alert.

A huge tongue of flames burst from the fire licking toward Tristan's feet. When the fire recoiled, a rolled parchment remained on the ground. He lifted it and read it aloud.

THE TREK back to their lands was done with as much haste as they'd begun. The missive from the Wizard in the flames claimed that they had three days before they'd be trapped in an enchantment.

The being had cast a curse upon them to be imprisoned in a different world unless freed by an enchantress that could break each of their specific spells.

If not saved, they'd be trapped in the alter-world forever.

Deep in thought, the men contemplated arrangements to make, goodbyes to say, and how to find someone who could save them from such a horrible fate.

Upon their arrival, they plunged into desperate, frantic searches for magicians, spellcasters, and witches—anyone who could save them from the dreadful fate looming over them. Panic gripped their every step, as they clung to the last thread of hope against the nightmare that awaited.

Chapter Fifteen

Derrick leaned back and read the papers in his hand. A business proposal, although a very attractive one, that didn't sit well with him. Across the desk from him sat William Montrose, CEO of the most prestigious hotels in Edinburgh and chairman at the Bank of Scotland.

Montrose, extremely well connected and wealthy, was just the type of person Derrick wanted to attract in the venture to turn McRainey Estates into a five-star resort. The problem: Montrose was also the competition.

"Lord McRainey, as you can see, our partnering would not only guarantee your establishment instant world-wide recognition, but put you on the list of 'must-see' places for the elite."

Montrose reached for his drink, allowing the words to sink in. His sharp gaze never left Derrick's face. "We propose a very lucrative sum, with the understanding that we will be in a partnership with no money involved, and not in competition. In other words, all business decisions will be coordinated between us to ensure the best outcome for us both."

"It's hard to see what I have to lose from this," Derrick answered, his eyes meeting Montrose's. "What I don't understand is what you have to gain."

The man did not answer right away. Derrick could sense his wheels turning, analyzing how to answer the question. "We'd gain from the lack of competition of course. Gleneagles is in a very strong position, but new resorts can entice our fickle clientele away."

A partnership agreement bonus was included for Derrick in the amount of several million pounds, once he signed. Derrick's pulse quickened as his eyes roved over the amount on the paperwork in front of him. With that amount, he could complete most of the golf course and building of the stables without having to touch his own money.

"I will certainly give your offer all due consideration Mr. Montrose." Derrick stood, letting his visitor know the meeting had ended, keeping the upper hand since they were on his home turf. Montrose's eyebrows lifted, not used to being dismissed. But he regained his composure and stood as well.

After the man left, Derrick let out a slow whistle while reading over the documents again. It seemed too good to be true, and as they said, what seemed too good... The intercom buzzed, interrupting his thoughts.

His secretary announced his aunt, and he slid the papers into the leather sleeve they'd been delivered in.

Edith entered, along with her the aroma of freshness and flowers, her favorite perfume. She sat without waiting for him to invite her to, very much at home, as this used to be her office. He genuinely liked his aunt; her strong sense for business propelled McRainey industries into one of the strongest corporations in Britain.

Their only point of contention was and always would be the future of the estate.

"Derrick, I must have a word with you regarding the workmen who've begun showing up at the estate," Edith began without preamble. "I know that on my eighty-fifth birthday you become the rightful owner, but that is still over a year away. I've sent them all away and will continue to do so until next June."

Pressing his lips together to keep from blurting out an angry expletive, Derrick nodded, his patience wearing thin. Her actions were costing him money.

"Aunt Edith, the changes will take place once I become the owner, which *will* happen come next June. You, more than anyone, understand the work must commence this year in order for the resort to be open to the public as soon as I secede you."

His aunt stood and rounded the desk; leaning over him she made the most of her five-foot-six stature. "Derrick, not one brick on my home will be touched until that last day in June. Do you understand?"

When he just stared at her and didn't reply, she continued. "I am confident Gwyneth will free Tristan McRainey and you will never inherit the estate. So save the money you are wasting on any plans for this 'public attraction' of yours."

With that she turned on her heel and stormed from the office.

Derrick's hand trembled as he loosened his tie, fighting the urge to run after her and demand she return and continue the discussion. However, no matter how angry his aunt made him, he would not disrespect the woman.

Tristan McRainey did exist—he was just a ghost, nothing more. The fable was untrue, he was not a captive of an enchantment.

True, he'd seen the apparition himself. As a matter of fact, his ancestor had been a sort of constant companion of his when he was a child. Once he grew up, he stopped seeing him.

As much as he felt a certain tie to the man, he didn't think it was fair to lose this opportunity to become the next Lord of McRainey Estates and forge his own legacy, all because of his aunt's fixation on a dead man.

And if he had to use Gwen Lockhart to win this contest, he'd do so.

He would ensure Gwen was kept busy and not given the opportunity to spend any time on *freeing* the ghost.

Chapter Sixteen

The Internet yielded very little information into the world of Tristan McRainey. It seemed that scholars did not find very much worthy of reporting and left a large span of history during his lifetime blank. Most of the information Gwen had gathered from Tristan could not be verified. Information could help with the spell, a spell usually hinged on one crucial thing or event.

Tristan had said that each of the trapped men was to be freed separately, and that each spell would be different for the knight in question. Perhaps she needed to ask questions of a more personal nature on his next visit.

Repeating the words she'd felt an impulse to write hadn't worked for them. She closed her eyes, opened her mind to the universe and chanted them several times.

Nothing happened, not even a stirring.

Letting out a long breath, she decided to try once again, this time not expecting anything, except for inspiration for other words to come. She repeated the words in her head.

Vanquish the shields of time
Remove the walls of deception
Arise the winds of change and move
Unleash the spell of old from its holder

At first her vision was foggy, but slowly an image became clear, and she rocked side to side, repeating the words.

It was a long, deliberate process, as the image seemed reluctant to form. Finally she made out what looked like a young child, a little girl, dark-haired and very slight, no more than six or seven years old. As the girl moved, so did a large shadow behind her. With frightened eyes, the child stumbled forward, looking around frantically. When Gwen could stand it no more, the child finally slid into the hollow of a tree. The shadow passed by, not harming her.

Scant seconds later, the girl left the safety of the tree and ran back in the direction she came, only to be seen by the shadow and chased again. A scream echoed in her mind and Gwen shrieked startled. Her eyes sprang open, and the vision was gone.

Who was the little girl? What did she have to do with Tristan's enchantment?

A rap on the door made her jump. Gwen straightened and called for the visitor to enter.

Expecting Edith, she was surprised when Derrick stood in the doorway. Dressed in a business suit, he cut a professional figure. The tailor-made jacket fit his wide shoulders perfectly. He strolled in and gave her a questioning look.

Gwen looked down at her leggings and t-shirt and

shrugged at him. "Yoga," she explained. "You, on the other hand, are dressed less comfortably, but very nice."

"Nonetheless, you are a lovely vision, and thank you." Derrick leaned in to kiss her, and she turned her face allowing him to kiss her cheek. His expression remained blank as he moved back. "I came to return the portrait, but Aunt Edith is not home. Do you know where she is?"

"She went to Edinburgh and won't return until tomorrow," Gwen replied, anxious to run downstairs to see the portrait. "She's gone to see about your Uncle Roan, who is in the hospital."

"Ah yes, of course," Derrick replied, frowning deeply and looking worried. "Uncle Roan has been ill for a very long time."

"I'm sorry," Gwen said. Finally she could wait no more. "Is the portrait back up? I must go see it." She dashed from the room, Derrick right behind her.

TRISTAN McRAINEY WAS UNDOUBTEDLY the most handsome man she'd ever made love with. A warm blush heated her face as she looked up at the portrait. This time he'd been captured wearing his tartan and sporran. Standing by the fireplace in the great room, he embodied every bit the laird of his clan and every bit a mouthwatering hunk. Gwen allowed her eyes to feast on every inch of the face on the canvas, before finally lowering her gaze to look down his muscular chest to his well-formed arms and hands. Oh those hands, what they could do.

"You never did say if this is the man you saw." Derrick interrupted her thoughts. "Have you seen him again?"

"He looks familiar," she stuttered. Okay stupid thing to say. "I mean, yes, of course it's him. Tristan McRainey. And yes, I saw him again, just yesterday."

"So this means you won't be leaving then." His eyes locked on her lips and Gwen felt uncomfortable, not just at Derrick's closeness, but that he flirted with her in front of Tristan's portrait.

"No. Yes, actually, I am leaving. I have to fly to America, but I'll be returning." She was going to get the book, but didn't want him to know that.

"Is it really necessary?" Derrick asked, not explaining if he meant her departure or her return.

"Yes, I have to see my sisters about a family matter," Gwen told him, not exactly lying, "and I do have to return. I will not give up until your aunt decides all that can be done has been done."

Running his hand down her arm in a slow deliberate manner that no doubt yielded him results with many women, Derrick gave her a lazy smile. "Do you honestly believe in the fairy tale, Gwyneth?"

"If I didn't believe in the spirit world, what kind of a medium would I be? Derrick, look—many doubt my profession. I am not bothered by it. I have helped the departed find their way home and families get the closure they utterly needed. I am very proud of my calling."

As she spoke, he moved closer. Gwen tried to take a step back, but she was cornered.

"Tea, sir?" The maid's voice was shrill. When Derrick

turned to glare at the intruder, Gwen took advantage and ducked past him into the sitting room.

"Thank you, Hannah," Derrick gave the maid a curt nod. "You may leave."

Hannah's eyes slid to Gwen. She didn't seem inclined to leave. "Do you require anything, miss?" she asked, her voice clipped.

"No, thank you. I will pour," Gwen replied. Glad to have something to do and put space between her and Derrick, she went to the tray, preparing to serve the tea.

"Very well," Hannah said, retreating.

Derrick ignored the teacup Gwen placed in front of him.

"I have to ask you to desist at once in your efforts to free Tristan McRainey."

"I can't do that."

"Of course you can. I haven't told you this before. The man was a murderer. If what you believe is true, do you want to release his like into our world? What of my aunt's safety? Do you not care about her well-being?"

Chapter Seventeen

"You didn't join us for the evening meal," Padraig said, planting himself directly in front of Tristan.

"Everything okay?" Padraig's use of modern English was a common occurrence, as he frequently visited his ancestral home, which was now divided into what Padraig called *apartments*.

The fact didn't seem to bother the young knight, who was forever entertained by the different people that moved in and out of the house. Of all of them, Padraig was the most in tune with current customs and language.

"Yes, I'm well. Would you please move aside, you're blocking my light." Tristan turned the page in the book he read and ignored Padraig's stare.

"Gavin and Liam fought. Liam attacked Gavin, effectively clearing the table of all of our food and dishes. You missed a good fight."

Padraig sank into a chair, and began to toss his dirk into

the air, catching it by the handle as it fell. "Are you leaving again tonight?"

Not able to concentrate, Tristan put his book aside after marking the page. "Yes, of course. I will go as often as I can. We are running out of time." He stretched and yawned.

He'd been sitting for hours, reading books he'd taken from his house over the years, books different people had brought to Edith in hopes of helping with the enchantment. He'd read each one many times over the years, each time hoping to find something he'd missed somehow.

Padraig, usually light of heart, seemed troubled. His anxious gaze looked past Tristan to the fireplace. "In two years the enchantment will end. One way or another, we'll finally be free."

"In death, there is freedom," Tristan replied, without emotion. "Paddy, we have lived almost four hundred years. Most would welcome death."

The young knight became angered. "We haven't *lived*, Tristan, we've been *existing*. In a state of suspended animation," his said, bright-blue eyes blazing.

"Anima... what?" Tristan shrugged. "Never mind, you're correct, we stopped living when we came here. Nonetheless, the outcome will be what fate decides—fret nor worry can change that."

"Have you told the enchantress about the deadline?"

"No, not yet. I see a sense of urgency in her. Gwyneth is working steadfastly towards finding the spell to break the enchantment."

"What of the other part? Are you working your wiles on the wench?" Padraig's humor returned.

Tristan shook his head but remained serious. "That, my friend, is the not going to be a problem. She is attracted to me. She has a hard time remaining aloof when I am present."

"Good," Padraig replied. "I wonder what her sacrifice is going to be."

"Let us not get ahead of ourselves. For now we must remain on alert. Meliot won't sit by idly, allowing me so much freedom."

As if on cue, the ground shook. Padraig went to the window. "Horses. From the sound of it, a large army approaches." Harnessing his magical powers, his eyes glowed and he spread his arms, sending pulses of energy from his palms, toward the protective magic wall.

"I must ensure the keep is well protected." The young knight flew from the room. Tristan followed to find the others.

The great room was full of activity when he entered, Niall and Gavin donning armor and strapping daggers to their bodies. Liam stood facing the fire, his pose still as he looked into the flames, seeking a vision.

Padraig rushed in, his long red hair loosened out of its strap from all the energy he'd expended. "They've surrounded the keep, about a hundred horsemen. From the looks of it, they are not approaching past the line of my ward. If they attack, it may not be until sundown."

"They won't attack." Liam turned to face them. Lines of worry etched around his mouth as he looked at Tristan. "They are here to ensure we do not leave the keep. We are trapped inside. So that we cannot will ourselves to the other side."

Anger shook him, and Tristan threw a chair across the room. Immediately he felt bad. Niall worked hard to make each piece of furniture, to give them a semblance of a normal home. He went to pick up the chair and assess the damage.

"We will figure out a way to get you out," Niall told him, taking the chair and then bending to pick up a leg that had broken off.

"This gives me something to do." He gave Tristan a rare smile.

Niall turned to Padraig. "Figure something out."

"Oookay, right. Like, why don't I just wave a fairy wand and magically transport us to the forest behind the hundreds of blood-thirsty killers out there." The men all stared at him, not speaking.

"Great idea," Liam exclaimed. "Great idea indeed."

At sundown, some hours later, the men were in a clearing inside the forest. Tristan studied each of the knights before him. They were the bravest men he'd ever had the honor of knowing. Dressed in full armor, he could only see their eyes. "I will try not to be long."

"We'll be here when you return," Gavin replied, and placed his hand on Tristan's shoulder. "Paddy will return us to the garden behind the keep; once we sense your return, we'll be here to meet you."

"Now go," Niall insisted.

Chapter Eighteen

On a table in her guestroom, a candlelit dinner for two was set. Once again, Gwen touched the top of the covered dish in the center of the small table to ensure it was warm. Anxious after her discussion with Derrick, she'd sought the comfort of the kitchen. Cooking always allowed her time to think and relax.

Two glasses of wine and a tasty Italian braised-chicken dish later, she felt ready to face Tristan. If he ever showed up.

Anxiety reared its ugly little head once again as she glanced at the clock on the mantel. It was almost eleven o'clock at night. Perhaps he couldn't get away. Meliot may have come up with another stall tactic so he couldn't will himself to the estate.

A low grumble of her stomach made her reach for a piece of bread. She'd written down the many questions she had for him. Most importantly, finding out what happened to his betrothed. Was he the one that had hunted and killed the little girl? She poured a glass of wine and sat at the table. "Might as well eat," she grumbled.

"An inviting picture. How did ye know I'd be hungry?" Tristan appeared just as she put a piece of chicken in her mouth. Butterflies fluttering in her chest, she motioned for him to sit.

He eyed the food and waited for her to fix his plate. She almost told him to serve himself, but then figured that in his time, as laird, he was used to being served. After she finished plating his chicken dish, he poured himself a glass of wine and took a sip. When his eyes met hers, he didn't flirt like he usually did.

"You seem preoccupied," Gwen told him. "Is something wrong?"

With a half-hearted shrug, he tasted the chicken, and his eyes widened. "This is delicious—the cook is very good."

"Thank you," Gwen smiled at his compliment, enjoying his realization that she had prepared the meal. "I enjoy cooking when I can. My mother owns a restaurant, er, an eating establishment."

He nodded but didn't speak while he ate, cleaning his plate. Then he eyed the serving dish. Gwen served him again.

"Tristan, I have written down some questions. Please continue to eat." She picked up her tablet, deciding to tackle the hardest question first.

"It is said that at the time of your disappearance you were betrothed. Is that true?"

Tristan took a swallow of wine and nodded. "Yes, to the MacDougal lass. We were to be married that spring."

He didn't seem disturbed at her mention of his fiancée, so she continued. "Do you know what happened to her?"

He chewed while in thought. His green eyes connected with hers. The heat in them had returned and Gwen looked away. It was either that or throw herself on top of him.

"She married my brother. He took over as laird, so it made sense. Her clan was anxious for the joining with ours."

Well, not that his words proved anything, but folklore usually came from facts. She believed him. She decided to move ahead and ask the next question.

"Did you have children? Sons or daughters?"

Tristan put down his fork, and this time he pondered his answer. Finally, when his eyes met hers, they were filled with sadness. "Yes, I did. I fathered two children out of wedlock. A boy and a girl. Both with the same woman. She was a villager whom I… visited frequently. Since my children had no rights to any of my holdings, I gifted their mother with a parcel of land and enough coin to provide for her until my children reached adulthood."

It was common for a laird to have bastard-born children, but it wasn't normal for them to take much interest in them. It seemed Tristan was very different.

"Did you love her?"

He didn't pretend not to know whom she referred to. "Mairéad was a fine woman… she was a friend. But no, I don't believe I loved her."

"Were you able to know how your children fared?"

Tristan stood and walked to the fireplace, his back to her. "Can we talk about something else? I don't believe my children's fate matters at this point."

Touchy subject.

Gwen cleared her throat and continued. "Did you ever see a young girl... lass in the forest, in distress?"

He turned, frowning, head cocked to the side. "How did ye know about that?"

Her stomach plummeted. "I had a vision of someone chasing a small girl in the woods."

For a long moment, he was silent. "My sister Mairi. She was killed. We found her body in the woods near here. We never knew who did it. Did ye see who it was that chased her?" He looked at her with expectation.

Although his explanation settled her, she felt bad for bringing it up and not giving him any answers. "No. But I can try, perhaps later. I don't think it's important at this moment.

"Tristan, I believe my spell as it stands is a good start, but I need to fetch my spell book to do further research. I am going to leave Scotland for a few days."

His eyes went wide, terrified. Gwen watched him fight to school his features into a neutral expression. "When are you leaving? Is it absolutely necessary?" He'd moved toward her, stopping only when she took his hand.

He needed to be reassured. Gwen stood and wrapped her arms around him. He allowed her to hold him, and bent to lay his cheek on top of her head.

"Don't go." The words were so soft, she wasn't sure he'd uttered them.

"I must, Tristan. I am so close to finding the correct words, but I'm missing something, I have to get my book."

"It's becoming harder for me to come. But I will find a

way to be here when you return." He pulled back to allow her to look at his face. Any sign of vulnerability was gone. The self-assured man stood before her.

She reached around his neck and pulled him down to her. Their lips collided with force, passion that only two people who were meant to be together could evoke. His mouth feasted on hers, while his hands made haste in removing her garments.

Not able to stand the barrier of clothing between them, Gwen began to pull at his, as well. She pushed him back on the bed, startling him, but he quickly recovered and held his arms up to her, an enticing invitation to be sure.

Instead of lying down, she knelt and took his shoes off. After pulling his breeches off, she massaged his thighs enjoying the view of his parted legs. Tristan hissed when she began to lick his inner thighs. His cock twitched back and forth, begging for her touch, but she resisted, instead she cupped his sack and licked the soft flesh. His moan told her he enjoyed her attentions.

Finally, she gave him what he wanted and took him fully in her mouth. Using her hand to cover the base, she allowed her lips to slide up and down his long, swollen member. Tristan bucked into her mouth, and she let him pump, sliding in and out between her lips, until he began losing control. She squeezed his sack, and he lost total control. With a loud growl, he came.

She waited until he finished trembling, and she slowly slid him out of her mouth. Panting, she slid up his body, her aching center needing his touch.

Not a man to allow her to do all the work, he flipped her

on her back and kissed her until she was breathless and begging for him to coax her over the edge. He slid two fingers inside her, while his thumb played havoc with her swollen center. Gwen pushed against his hand. He seemed to time it perfectly and just as she was about to come, he'd stop his movements smiling wickedly at her.

"Damn it Tristan, don't stop," Gwen cried, on the verge of actual tears.

When his revived shaft slipped into her, she kicked and screamed as thousands of stars exploded behind her eyelids. He waited for her to settle and then began to coax her into another climb, with him this time. The frantic sounds of their lovemaking reached fevered heights as both took turns slamming into each other, first him, then she flipped him and rode him until almost collapsing. At which point, he rolled her back over and pulling her legs up over his shoulders, he carried them over the crest, sending them both screaming into orgasm.

Fully sated seemed to barely describe how she felt as she studied the man lying next to her with his arm behind his head and his other hand holding hers. She couldn't help but wonder if he was as good in bed before he'd had hundreds of years to practice. She sat up at the thought.

"Are there women in the alter-world?"

He gave her a puzzled look. "No, there are no other humans. Why?"

She blushed, but ignored her reaction to feeling jealous at the thought that he had lovers in the alter-world. "What do you guys do for sexual release?"

Tristan's lips curved, amused. "We are forced to take care

of ourselves for the most part. Until I met you, I couldn't remain here long enough to do much more than perhaps steal a kiss."

"Wow, and I thought *I* went a long time between lovers," Gwen replied. Her comment was greeted by a low growl and dark expression.

"Ye will have no other lover than me." It was a statement, an order, no room for discussion it seemed.

"Not that you need to hear this, but I can't even think about anyone else, not after this." She motioned to his private area. "You are amazing in bed."

Tristan didn't preen as she expected, instead, he frowned at her. "There is more to me than just... this." He pointed to the same area.

He rolled over and faced her, his nose inches from hers. "I want to get to know you." He kissed her.

They kissed for a long time. Gwen could feel him hardening again, but he didn't move to make love to her. He pressed his lips to her ear. "Do you think you can grow to love me, fair Gwyneth?"

Gwen cupped his jaw and turned his face to hers, looking into his eyes. "If ever there was someone I could fall in love with, you are he."

If only he wasn't whatever he was.

His green gaze held hers for a few moments. When he spoke, Gwen felt like the luckiest woman to ever walk the earth.

"That is good, because I do not want to be the only one falling in love."

This time their mouths and bodies met until once again they made love with a slower rhythm of lovemaking.

Chapter Nineteen

In love? Of course not. Tristan was not in love with her, and she wasn't in love with him. It was after-sex talk... yes, definitely. After all, what could they possibly base any kind of feelings on? Well, other than the fact that she admired his courage and honor. She liked his ability to make her feel special, and how he bravely defied the odds to try and find freedom not just for himself, but the other men. She had to admit, she found him irresistible and couldn't stop thinking about him. Loved how their conversations trailed off into comfortable silences. Then there was the chemistry, totally through the roof. Yes, definitely, not love.

When the seatbelt light finally blinked off, Gwen jumped out of her seat, her carry-on satchel already in-hand, and shuffled quickly off the plane. Spotting her sisters first, she dashed towards them. If only she'd asked them to meet her with the book, so she could turn around and fly straight back.

"Oh God," Tammie exclaimed, jumping up and down, her ponytail swinging back and forth. "She's in love!"

"What?" Gwen stumbled losing her balance. Sabrina reached out and steadied her.

Both sisters studied her briefly. Sabrina nodded. "Yes, I believe you're correct Tammie, our little girl is head over heels."

"How long have you two been at the airport, because you've obviously hit a bar or two?" Gwen asked them, hugging each, before they made their way out to the parking lot. "I've only been in Scotland two weeks. Barely enough time to fall in lust." Her laugh rang hollow.

Tammie linked an arm through hers and leaned into her. "Is it Derrick McRainey? Please say no. He is a well-known player who's still got a few years before he settles down."

When Sabrina stepped to her other side and took her bag, then joined arms with her as well, a sigh escaped Gwen.

"We need to know the details, every itty-bitty detail of what this man has done to make our overly cautious sister fall so hard and so fast." Sometimes having two sisters with special gifts could be a pain.

Thankfully, the inquisition stopped until they reached Sabrina's sleek silver Mercedes.

Sabrina, a successful photographer who specialized in shooting male models for high-fashion magazines and ad campaigns, collected cars like most women collected purses. Right now she owned three, including a Jaguar, a Jeep, and the Mercedes.

Sliding into the back seat, Gwen took a deep breath and

didn't wait for her sisters to bombard her with questions. She decided to speak first.

"I am not in love, at least I hope I'm not. The man in question is a great guy, brave, handsome, caring, great in bed, and seems to care for me as well." She smiled at her sisters' jaw-popping expressions.

"So why are you not excited? Why didn't you bring him with you? How could you bear to be separated from Mr. Wonderful?" Tammie exclaimed, dramatically clutching her hand over her heart.

"Well, he can't exactly leave the country," Gwen hedged. "He isn't happy about me leaving Scotland, that's for sure."

"Who is he, already?" Sabrina's eyes met hers in the rear-view mirror.

Gwen didn't get a chance to reply, because the Mercedes swerved sharply, coming to a stop so abruptly the car rocked back and forth several times before finally stopping completely.

Tammie screamed and hit Sabrina on the shoulder. "Are you trying to kill us?"

Gwen fell across the back seat laughing hard, not sure when it turned sobbing until Sabrina climbed into the back seat and began to soothe her.

Tammie twisted around giving them a confused look. "What am I missing? What happened?"

"Shh," Sabrina replied patting Gwen's back. "Gwen's in love with McRainey."

"Oh," Tammie replied. "Oh, I'm sorry, honey, maybe he's not that much of a playboy. Maybe you'll be the one to settle him down."

"Not that McRainey," Sabrina hissed.

"Oh. My. God." Tammie shrieked, "She's in love with the dead guy?"

BACK AT THEIR large townhouse in Buckhead, Gwen sat on a stool in the kitchen drinking a glass of wine, while her sisters pretended to keep busy. Interesting that both of them found so much to do in the same room as her.

Sabrina tossed a salad, Tammie whipped up salad dressing, while talking on her cell phone. She was in the process of canceling her plans for the evening. Her evening plans must have been complicated, because she made a third phone call.

"You don't have to stay home," Gwen told her youngest sister again. "There is really nothing to tell."

"Oh no, you're so sharing, and we are going to help you free that man," Tammie told her, her bangs bouncing with every word. "You're in love, for the first time ever. We can't waste any time."

"She's right," Sabrina piped in, carrying the salad to the table. "We'll discuss the facts over dinner. As soon as we eat, we're going to begin going through the spell book and find the right spell to break the enchantment. If that doesn't work, we'll call in the big gun." She referred to their mother, Iona.

Gwen didn't argue. One thing about the Lockhart sisters, as different as they were in appearance, they were identical when it came to their stubborn streaks.

As Tammie began to set the table, she paused, her brow

pinched. "Gwen, did Tristan say what you had to do, after chanting the spell, to break the enchantment?"

"He said something about a sacrifice. Giving up something dear, something hard to part with. I asked him who had to do that part. He said, it would be clear once the time came. I think it's him, but I'm not so sure." Gwen dug her journal out of her large satchel. "I've already written a spell. It seems right, but something is missing."

"Come sit down," Sabrina told her, pushing a bright-red tendril behind her ear before lifting a platter of steaming risotto and peas and putting it on the table.

"What do you think?" Gwen asked, after reading her spell to her sisters.

"It sounds right. I sense emotion has to be put into it," Sabrina said, sitting back, her wine glass in hand. "Add a sentence, like Mom always says, like "Be now evermore."

"I can't believe I forgot that." Gwen exclaimed, scribbling it into the spell, she began to chant it, but Tammie jumped up and stopped her.

"Don't! If it works, you're too far away to do whatever comes next."

THE SISTERS STAYED up late into the night, going over every piece of Gwen's notes. She didn't share her time with Tristan in bed with as much detail, but told them enough that they understood how compatible they were in lovemaking.

Tired, but not wanting to give up, Gwen flipped through the pages of the spell book, then stopped abruptly when reaching a passage that referred to Meliot. Her eyes widened seeing a depiction of the wizard. "This is him."

Both sisters peered over her shoulders.

"He's evil-looking," Tammie whispered. "Beady eyes."

"I think he looks like a grumpy old man," Sabrina said, her voice low.

"Well, he is evil, and has trapped Tristan and the other four knights for almost four hundred years. And he does have beady eyes," Gwen agreed, shuddering.

"According to the book, he's a powerful bugger, but needs to procreate in order to stay powerful. It is a rare occasion that the window opens for him to trap women through which he hopes to father boys who would help him take more power." Gwen shuddered,

"Ewwww!" Tammie put her hand over her mouth. "That's gross."

"He almost did it, until Tristan and the others rescued the young women when they defended that village."

"I wonder why he didn't just go back to get them later?" Tammie asked.

"Tristan said the timing had to be just right, and I think the wizard needed some sort of preparation. Knowing how magic works, he probably had to perform some type of ceremony or ritual. After the rescue it was too late to do his evil deed."

"Oh God," Sabrina paled, "I think I know what the sacrifice is going to be."

The knot in her stomach made Gwen afraid to ask.

"What?" Gwen finally asked.

"The sacrifice could have something to do with Tristan's

kids. I'm willing to bet Meliot has them and since Tristan took away from the wizard the ability to have children..." Sabrina didn't finish.

"Oh no," Gwen gasped. "That would be terrible. I hope you're wrong."

"Well, if he's the one to sacrifice something then I'm sure I'm right. However, if you're the one to sacrifice something, then it could be something totally different."

"Me? You think I may have to be the one to give up something?"

"Like Tristan McRainey said, it will come clear once the time comes."

"I'm heading back tomorrow." Gwen closed the spell book. "I'd appreciate it if one of you came with me."

Tammie shook her head. "I can't, I have an opening at the Bennett Art Gallery—it starts tomorrow night. I can fly over next week."

"I'll do it." Sabrina placed her hand over Gwen's. "I have a Marc Jacobs photo shoot coming up soon. Why not scout Scotland for the perfect location?"

"I can't believe how lucky I am to have you two in my life," Gwen stated, blinking away tears.

"Oh Soppy, stop it," Tammie grinned, giving her a stern look, her shiny eyes giving away the fact that she felt the same.

Sabrina let out a loud laugh. "I'll go pack and then we're off to rescue the hunky man in distress!"

Chapter Twenty

Brooding was not something he was prone to do. But for the last two days, that's exactly what he'd done. Discontented at his mood, Tristan mulled over his last conversation with Gwen. Not quite sure of the emotion that tickled the corners of his conscious, but it felt like guilt. He'd done what he had to do and planted the seed, the thought of falling in love. He had no choice. In order for the enchantment to be broken the enchantress had to fall in love with him. That the guilt seemed overshadowed by another emotion pulled him into the dark mood. When he'd told Gwen he didn't want to be the only one falling in love, it wasn't exactly a lie. His heart had jumped, his voice hitched, a lump caught in his throat.

"Bah," he snorted, and moved toward the window to peer out to see if the horsemen remained. They did.

When he became a free man, able to live a normal human life in the modern world, how could he possibly hope to attain a woman like Gwyneth Lockhart? Independent, self-sufficient, and powerful in her own right. He was not much more than a barbarian, compared to the men of her time. There were so many things he didn't know about her world, so many changes had taken place since he'd left. What could he possibly have to offer her?

Wealth. As far as he knew, the family had taken very good care of the McRainey fortune, which made him a rich man. He'd secreted away gold in the keep before leaving. It remained there, hidden in a cave under the cellar, worth quite a bit more now. Still, a woman like Gwen was not swayed by riches.

What did it matter? He'd regain his life. He'd have his hands full, relearning to run the estate. Perhaps in time, he'd meet someone, after he became accustomed to modern life. The thought of spending time with a woman other than Gwen didn't sit well.

"Well I'll be damned," Tristan whispered.

Feeling the now familiar pull, he knew Gwen was back. He glanced out the window one last time, the lines of horsemen a menacing view. Campfires dotted the lands surrounding the keep. *How long would they remain?*

In the great room, Liam and Niall sat at the long trestle table with a chess set between them while Gavin paced in front of the fireplace. Tristan noticed that the chess players were not actually playing.

"Has Paddy not returned?" Tristan asked, automatically scanning the room for the young Irishman.

"Nay," Niall replied. "It's been too long since he vanished to the clearing." Padraig had gone to scout the area prior to moving them there to help Tristan leap to the other side. He'd left against Niall's orders.

"I'll go check on him," Tristan told Gavin, who seemed poised to do just that. "I'm the reason he's in trouble, so it falls on me to help him. I might as well use some of this pent-up energy on something useful."

"The lass may have something to say about a use for your 'energy.'" Liam gave him a double eyebrow wag. "I can go check on the young lad."

"No, I will go," Gavin said, ignoring Liam's indignant growl.

Before they could argue further, Tristan ran out back to the walled garden and willed himself to the clearing. As soon as he materialized, he was attacked by four enormous warriors. Soulless, the lot of them, their empty black eyes totally hollow as they swung their cleavers and battle-axes. Tristan did not see Padraig but had little time to ponder it. He began fighting with all his might. When four additional warriors appeared and threw themselves at him, sending him falling to the ground, he pulled from his power of strength and flung them off. No sooner did they land on the ground than they turned around and pounced back on top of him.

He managed to cut two down and began backing up. He needed space to will himself away, and they were not giving an inch.

The clank of metal fastening around his left wrist startled him. One of the warriors yanked at the chain and held fast. Tristan swung his arm around and sent the idiot flying into nearby trees. Catching the chain, another two pulled him down to the ground again. This time he rolled, but before he could stand, another cuff was snapped on his right wrist. Tristan howled in anger, he pulled the chains out of the warriors' clasps and knocked one out, swinging the chains, using them as weapons as he inched away.

Getting enough space, he willed himself to Gwen.

Nothing happened. The cuffs were magic.

No doubt belonged to Meliot. When a strike to the back of his head drove him to his knees, Tristan could not swing hard enough to stop the second blow, the one that plunged him into darkness.

PAIN WAS AN INTERESTING THING. For hours he'd howled in pain at the henchmen's torture. Now, Tristan saw the falling of the metal bar and heard the crunch of his knee when the bones shattered, but he felt nothing, not anymore.

How long had he been here? He'd lost consciousness too many times to count, and each time he woke, the view was exactly the same, semi-darkness. Only a weak flicker of candles in a holder against the wall lightening the room, just enough for the henchmen to find their tool of choice.

He tried to speak but could only moan. His tongue dry and sluggish in the heat of his fevered mouth. When he tried to lift his head, it proved impossible. Death wasn't even something he could look forward to; Meliot would not allow him the respite. Not yet.

"Give him some water," Meliot loomed over him, studying his face. "Tristan." The wizard's bored expression made him wish he could laugh. "I hear you put up quite a fight in the forest. You can't fight much now, can you?"

Tristan closed his eyes as cool water poured down his throat, and once again tried to will himself away, but nothing happened.

"Did you really think I'd allow you to go free?" Meliot sneered. "It's almost time for my mating. My sons will rule Europe and who knows? Maybe the world. I won't take any chances this time.

"I think I'll keep you for a few months. Eventually the enchantress will become bored and leave."

Tristan felt a pang in his chest, this one rawer than the physical pain.

Meliot knew everything. What a fool he'd been to think the wizard was not aware of their comings and goings. He'd been ready to act when and if it became possible for them to find freedom.

The sad thing was, the wizard was probably right. Gwen would not wait long for him.

Liam jumped at Paddy's appearance. He looked worse for wear, bloody and breathing heavily.

"Bloody Hell," Liam exclaimed, as Niall reached the young Irishman, and began checking him for injuries. "You barely missed Tristan."

"Shit," Padraig shrugged away from Niall. "I'm not injured, the blood's not mine. At least I don't think it is. They were waiting for me. We can't use the clearing." He looked around noting Tristan's absence. "Where's McRainey?"

Liam exchanged a look with the other two men. "No doubt Meliot has him by now."

"I'll go challenge the bastard," Padraig told them. "He's not supposed to separate us."

"He plays by his own rules," Gavin told the young knight, then locking gazes with the other men. "One of us alone is not strong enough to face Meliot. Tristan needs help."

"What are you going to do, Campbell?" Liam sneered. "Seduce the wizard into giving you McRainey?"

"Shut up Liam." Gavin didn't spare him a glance. "I'm going to get help. I'll fetch the lass. Gwyneth Lockhart's destiny is coming to pass. She must do her part."

Chapter Twenty-One

"From what I can tell, this is a colossal waste of time, energy, and money," Derrick told the women, who'd been subjected to his rants for the last half hour. "Don't take offense Gwen, but you have to agree, not one bit of progress has been made in the endeavor to 'free' Tristan McRainey." He made air quotes before continuing. "It's time to accept reality. The ghost, if there ever was one, is gone."

"I don't agree," Edith began, "something is detaining Laird McRainey, something unavoidable, otherwise he'd have appeared by now." She gave Gwen a weak smile. "Please don't let Derrick ruin your appetite dear. Eat."

Gwen tried to smile back at Edith, but it had been a horrible time since returning from Georgia. After two days of Tristan not appearing, she was beginning to wonder if she'd made a mistake by leaving, breaking some sort of tie between them. Sabrina still believed it held and so did Edith, but

Derrick's rantings were increasingly grating on her already frayed nerves.

"I think something is wrong. Otherwise he'd have appeared by now." She pierced a piece of roast with her fork and brought it to her mouth. What if Tristan was in trouble, suffering, hurt, in Meliot's clutches? She put the food back down, appetite lost.

"We'll wait," Sabrina assured her. She addressed Derrick. "My sister is very good at what she does. If she says Tristan McRainey is real, then he is. I don't see how the outcome of this will affect you; whether he's real or not, your life will continue as usual. You're wealthy enough that you can build a new resort from scratch, are you not?"

"Sabrina!" Gwen exclaimed, contrite at her sister's directness.

"No, that's quite alright," Derrick replied, his angry gaze locked on Sabrina. "You are correct, Miss Lockhart, I am wealthy in my own right. If I believed my ancestor were truly a trapped man, then of course I'd want him to be freed from this curse. If that's what's happening. What I won't do is stand by idly and allow my aunt to spend her money on an unnecessary pursuit."

"No charge," Gwen retorted, now losing her temper with the insolent man. "I won't accept one red cent for freeing Tristan."

Derrick raised an eyebrow. "Tristan? Are you on a first-name basis with the ghost?"

"Enough," Edith interrupted, in a soft, stern voice. "Please let's retire to the sitting room for a glass of brandy. I think we need it."

Once in the sitting room, Derrick poured them all a drink while Edith spoke. "The matter of Miss Lockhart's employment is not up for discussion. I am of sound mind and will decide when and if we will cease in this pursuit. I believe you are swayed by your desire to take over the estate and transform it into that distasteful public attraction of yours." She rolled her eyes at Derrick, who reddened but remained silent. "I am not required to hand over management of the estate until my eighty-fifth birthday, which isn't for another year, dear nephew. Until the last day of June, next year, I will remain steadfast in my decision to do anything I can to free Tristan McRainey."

Gwen didn't dare argue, but she'd made up her mind. She was not accepting any payment for working on Tristan's release. It was now a personal quest.

Once Derrick left, Gwen got up and poured the women a second drink. "I meant what I said Edith. I don't require payment of any kind. I want to do this."

Edith reached for her glass and smiled at her. "In love, are you?"

Sabrina let out a loud laugh. Gwen's face grew hot.

"Why is everyone saying that?" She sputtered, not enjoying that Edith joined in Sabrina's laughter. "I like him. Of course he's very handsome—who wouldn't find him attractive..." She gave up and fell on the chair shaking her head; they weren't listening to her anyway.

Edith sobered first. "I'm sorry dear, but we have to find

humor where we can. I am worried about Tristan, too. What could possibly be detaining him?"

"Tristan McRainey needs yer help, lass," a deep voice shocked them.

They were struck silent as the man, who'd suddenly appeared, moved toward them. To say the man was a beautiful creature was a total and utter understatement. The golden warrior stood before them, his heavily lashed, honey-colored eyes scanning their faces, waiting for some sort of reply. Golden waves framed his face and fell to his wide shoulders. Dressed in soft leather britches and a belted white linen shirt with a huge sword on his hip, he embodied every woman's dream of what a warrior should look like. Muscles rippled on his huge frame as he moved to get a closer look at her. Despite his large size, he was as graceful as he was gorgeous. Until he tripped on the carpet and almost fell face first on top of her. She held her arms up, glad the huge man had managed to stop his fall.

Gwen finally was able to speak. "You must be Gavin Campbell."

He nodded, the golden waves of his hair fell forward, and he brushed his hair back, an impatient gesture. "I came to fetch ye, Gwyneth. You must come to the alter-world with me."

Gwen gasped. "What happened to Tristan?"

Gavin's eyes flickered to Sabrina. He hesitated for a second before returning his attention to Gwen. "Meliot has taken him. Ye must come and help Padraig. Only by combining your magic, can we stand a chance against Meliot."

"Well I'm not sure about this," Edith began, standing up to the large man. She didn't seem as affected by his looks. "Look here, Campbell, let's discuss this before you go off with Gwen. How do we know you are who you say." She finished by pushing a bony finger at his bicep. "Prove who you are."

The Scot gave Edith an incredulous look before he began untying the laces to the front of his shirt.

"Oh, this is going to be good," Sabrina whispered at Gwen, taking a sip of her brandy, her eyes glued to the Scot's chest. "Take it off, baby."

"Be quiet, Sabrina," Gwen hissed at her sister, who gave her a wicked smile in response.

"I believe this should prove who I am," Gavin told them, pulling out a talisman that matched Tristan's, except this one had a heart stamped on it, not a clover.

"Well, that was a letdown," Sabrina muttered, leaning forward to study the talisman. Gwen noticed that Gavin tensed, leaning away from her sister. *Interesting.*

Gwen reached for the talisman; she had to stand on her toes to see it more closely since it hung from a leather strap around Gavin's neck. His golden eyes studied her while he waited for her to decide.

"How are you able to come here?" Gwen asked, "I thought each of you could only appear at your ancestral homes."

He shrugged, "I never tried to come here until today. In the past, I have not been successful in appearing anywhere but Castle Campbell. I visited McRainey lands once before the enchantment. Tristan and I are childhood friends. Perhaps that is why I can."

"Let me get a jacket and the book." Gwen dashed out of the room. She wasn't surprised when Sabrina followed her.

"I know what you're going to say, but I have to go." She ran into her bedroom and pulled a heavy denim jacket from her closet. She sat on the bed and pulled on hiking boots as Sabrina shoved the spell book into a knapsack.

She eyed her sister who rushed about and continued shoving items into the bag. "Sabrina what all are you stuffing into that bag?"

"I'm not going to try to convince you not to go. It's useless. Not sure what you may need, so I'm adding some energy bars, Chap Stick, tampons, and sanitizer wipes. Also, a couple pairs of clean panties, two pairs of socks and lastly this extra t-shirt." Sabrina rolled the shirt and slid it into the deceptively small bag.

Grabbing the bag from her sister, Gwen hurried back to the great room. No telling how long Gavin could remain before being pulled back to the alter-world.

Once again, she was struck silent when she saw Gavin. As much as she preferred Tristan, it was almost impossible not to gawk at the man.

Sabrina nudged Gwen's shoulder with her own. "Yeah, I know. I would love to do a photo shoot. This guy is beyond words. I see a lot of great-looking men on a regular basis, but never someone like him. He just takes your breath away." She groaned. "Oh the money he could make with that face."

Gavin came over after nodding in deference to Edith. "Are ye ready to go?" He gave Sabrina a curious look, his handsome face frowning at how intently she watched him. No doubt she was picturing him in many different settings, her photographer's brain humming. "Are ye an enchantress as well?"

"Oh no, I mean, well, I haven't practiced. I help Gwen do research." She narrowed her eyes at him. "Why?"

"Perhaps you can help another one of us leave the enchantment." He placed his hand on her shoulder and cocked his head to the side. "I do not feel anything; perhaps, I am not the knight you can help."

Sabrina's lips parted, her breathing coming in short pants. She shoved his hand away. "Yeah, well I don't feel anything either."

Gavin turned to Gwen, "You must be prepared. As soon as we arrive, Padraig will be waiting for us. He will take you to the keep."

"What about you?" Gwen asked, as he wrapped his arms around her. He didn't reply.

"Close yer eyes, Gwyneth."

She peeked from under his arm at her sister. "See you soon."

At once, the air seemed to change, and she felt as if she were on a merry-go-round. A merry-go-round on steroids, spinning so fast she could only see blurs of different colors flash past. Her stomach heaved and she gagged, shutting her eyes and clutching desperately onto Gavin's large body.

She felt his warm breath in her ear as he spoke. "I told ye to keep yer eyes closed."

Solid ground finally. They slammed to a stop so fast that Gwen barely was able to stumble a couple of steps before she threw up. She bent over, holding on to a tree waiting for the dizziness to stop. A moan caught her attention, Gavin writhed on the ground, his teeth clenched, tears pouring down his face. He seemed to be in agony. A dark-haired male bent over him placing his hands on both shoulders.

She shuddered. He looked to be dying. "What's happening to him?"

The dark-haired man, who had to be Niall, the healer, didn't reply. He looked over at a younger male who stood by her and nodded. The young male smiled at her. "He'll be all right in a few secs, but we have to go." He held his hand out to her. "I'm Padraig."

As soon as Gwen touched his hand, they moved through space again. This time she kept her eyes tightly shut.

"You can open your eyes now," Padraig told her.

She'd pictured the knights' keep many times when Tristan had described it to her. The large stone fortress loomed before them. Behind it, the sky was purple, with two large suns shining down, casting violet and pinkish rays. Dashing inside, they entered a large room. The room was simply furnished, with pieces fashioned from earlier times, probably from their time. A large table surrounded by six beautifully carved chairs filled the center of the room. Against one wall, an enormous fireplace was flanked by two bookcases overspilling with books. Across from the fireplace stood a large sideboard with only a chess set on top. There were no wall decorations, the only warmth provided by animal skins strewn about.

A sleek male sat at the table, his cool eyes studying her. Padraig nodded towards him. "That's Liam."

"Hello." Gwen didn't move, still waiting for her uneasy stomach to settle.

"Hello Gwyneth. Welcome." Liam's accent reminded her he was English.

Liam jumped to his feet when Niall appeared, an unconscious Gavin over his shoulder. Although Niall was also a large man, he wasn't as large as Gavin. It impressed her, how easily he carried Gavin out of the room and up a stairway, Liam following right behind them.

Chapter Twenty-Two

"Should we go see if we can help?" Gwen asked Padraig, who watched Niall go upstairs, the still unconscious Gavin over his shoulder.

"Niall will take care of him," Padraig replied, his expression troubled. "Gavin had to leap twice to get to you. It's painful enough for us to leap once."

"You and Niall don't seem affected."

"We stayed here, in the same realm. He had to leap far to avoid the watchdogs outside, then again to your world. We expected this." Padraig went to the bookcases and pulled out several books. "Come on; let's get to work on Tristan's rescue."

Gwen followed him to the table. "I don't have any idea how to help you. I've never done anything like this before." She hated to ask, but felt compelled to. "What do you think is happening to Tristan?"

Padraig didn't look up. Taking a deep breath, he pressed his lips together, probably trying to figure out how to word his response. "Meliot will not hesitate to use any means necessary to inflict pain. About a hundred years back, for a long period he threw us into his dungeons. His torture regime is creative to say the least."

Anger flashed in the young knight's eyes, darkening them. It was obvious that recalling his time there still affected him. "The sooner we're able to get to Tristan, the better. I can guarantee you, he's not having a good time of it."

Gwen pulled her spell book out of her satchel. It slipped out of her hands, landing on the table, falling open. Both leaned in to read the spell on the page. It was a vanishing spell. Padraig grinned. "I see how that can work."

SEVERAL HOURS LATER, an exhausted Gwen leaned back and wiped her brow with her sleeve. "This is hard," she told Padraig. "I'm getting it, but I have to be able to vanish for longer if I'm going to be any help to Tristan."

"Let's try again. This time reach deeper inside, look for a bright red light, reach for it and hold on," Padraig said.

Chanting together, his deeper voice melding with hers, she saw the light. She used her mind to reach for it and suddenly it enveloped her. Breathing evenly, she felt the light enter her, and then it fully encompassed her, filling her with warmth.

"It's working," Padraig's whispered. "Open your eyes, if you haven't yet."

Nothing. She saw absolutely nothing in front of her. Padraig's hands were still linked with hers and she wanted to whoop in excitement. They'd done it.

They were totally invisible.

"Shhh," Padraig's voice hushed her. She turned to see Niall and Liam coming back down the stairs.

"Where did they go?" Liam asked Niall, who didn't reply but looked around the room, his gaze pausing on the open books on the table.

"Paddy knows he's supposed to tell us prior to going anywhere, especially to the wizard's castle." Liam continued.

Again Niall remained silent, his eyes narrowing as he scanned the room. Gwen bit her lip to keep from making a noise. They were truly invisible.

"They're here," Niall told the other man. "Not sure why I know, but I can sense someone here in the room."

Liam pulled out his sword,, his eyes searching the room. "Put that away," Niall told him.

Padraig squeezed Gwen's hand and whispered. "I think we better make ourselves visible before Liam slices and dices us."

When they appeared, Liam's eyes widened. He sheathed his sword and shook his head. "What were you thinking, Paddy? I could have hurt her."

"We weren't about to move," Padraig retorted, "Besides, why did you pull out your sword? Niall told you it was us."

The English knight frowned, not replying.

"How is Gavin?" Gwen asked the somber Irishman. "Can I see him?"

Niall nodded and motioned for her to follow him upstairs. As she made her way upstairs, she noted the hallways were well lit, but she didn't see electric fixtures or torches. It must be kept lit by Padraig's magic.

When they reached Gavin's room, Niall moved aside so she could enter. "He's awake, but verra weak right now. He will recover fully once he rests overnight." Niall's grey eyes glanced into the room, but he didn't go inside. As Gwen crossed the threshold, Niall left.

Gavin lay on the bed, his eyes open. He raised a questioning eyebrow at her appearance, but didn't say anything. Even pale, he looked like a prince in repose.

"I just came to make sure you were all right. If there's anything I can do..."

"Ye can concentrate on getting Tristan free," he replied, his voice strong. "Thank ye." He closed his eyes, turning away, effectively letting her know she'd been dismissed. Not wanting to bother him, she turned to walk out of the room, but stopped short when a small portrait caught her attention. She looked back to Gavin. He seemed to have fallen asleep. She stepped closer to the table at the side of the bed. The miniature was of a couple, a man whose looks resembled Gavin, same blond hair, wide shoulders; next to him, a beautiful woman, her thickly lashed amber eyes a legacy she passed to Gavin. His parents.

On a piece of paper next to the table were notes. She saw the name Sabrina, underlined. Interesting.

Why did he say he didn't feel anything when touching her? The answer was simple.

He'd lied.

Gwen didn't know what to make of her discovery; she pondered it on her way back to the great room. Perhaps after this was over, she'd question Gavin.

• • •

THE MEN LOOKED up when she walked down the stairs, ceasing whatever conversation they were having. Padraig held her knapsack out to her. She noticed the book of spells was no longer on the table.

"It's time. Niall will give you some extra strength. You'll need it."

Nodding, she took the knapsack. Niall laid his hands on their shoulders. Warmth radiated through her, like the feeling one got when submerging in a warm bath, her arms and legs loosened, and her muscles twitched, the feeling quite pleasant. When he removed his hand, she almost pleaded for him to touch her again.

"Thanks, Niall," Padraig nodded at the somber male. "Three of us will return shortly." With that, he took Gwen's hand, and they leapt back to the small clearing.

Once there, they leapt again.

This time they landed right in the center of hell.

Chapter Twenty-Three

Nude, on a wooden slab, legs apart, ankles shackled, his wrists bound above his head, the sense of helplessness filled him with fury.

How long had he been here? Days? Weeks? Tristan heard footsteps followed by the sound of two male voices.

"Is it time to wake him up again?"

"Yes."

"How long is he going to keep this one?"

"It's not our place to ask, or to care."

"So we are mindless drones that sit, beg, and roll over? That's not what I signed up for. Where's all the power I was promised?"

An unhappy recruit, Good to know.

"Shut up and hand me the needle.'"

"Fuck you."

Tristan peeked through half-closed eyes to see two men struggle over the injector. The larger one, an olive-skinned male, bashed the smaller man's head into the wall. When he slid limply to the floor, the larger of the two walked toward Tristan

"Are ye awake?" The man spoke in a soft whisper. Tristan opened his eyes. "What did you do to anger Meliot so?"

"Wrong place, wrong time," Tristan whispered, his voice almost gone from hours of screaming and nothing to drink. "Can I have some water?"

The man shrugged and brought over a ladle full of water. Lifting Tristan's head, he helped him drink it, refilled it twice, until he'd had his fill.

"Why did you hit him?" Tristan asked referring to the person on the floor.

"He's an idiot, I'm tired of hearing his bullshit," came the reply, as he studied Tristan.

"Like what you see?"

"I don't swing that way," the male replied, his cheeks coloring. From his contemporary speech, Tristan knew he was from modern times.

"I'm supposed to heal you enough so that you can withstand the next round with Meliot."

A *healer*.

The man walked over and laid his hands on Tristan's ribs. Instantly, warmth crept through him. His body bucked up from the table when a powerful bolt of energy surged into him. The male's eyes locked on to his private area.

From the hungry look, Tristan knew he'd lied. The male was very interested in what he saw. Maybe he could use it to his advantage.

His gut wrenched at the thought. He'd never once been attracted to men.

Once everything began to settle, he took a deep breath. For the first time in days, his ribs were fully healed.

"Thank you," Tristan locked gazes with the man, who looked away, reddening slightly. "What now?"

"I'll get Meliot." He didn't move.

"Who are you?"

"I'm Ryan."

"Have you been watching Meliot torture me?"

Once again Ryan's eyes flashed across his body. "Sometimes."

"Will you torture me?"

Ryan's discomfort radiated from him. He was not cut out to be one of Meliot's henchmen.

"I don't think so." The man turned to walk out.

"Wait."

Ryan hesitated but didn't turn.

Tristan scrambled for a way to stop him. "Do you want to touch me?"

This time Ryan turned. His eyes flashed, angry, but at the same time they locked on to Tristan's mouth. "What the fuck?"

"I know you want to." Tristan told him, forcing his eyes to linger at the male's mouth. "I'm right, aren't I?"

Ryan's hands clenched at his side, he glanced to the man on the floor before answering. "Yeah. Fine. You're right." He locked gazes with him, but didn't move. Slowly he dragged his eyes away from Tristan. "But I'm not stupid."

Torn between relief at not having to follow through and disappointment at not being able to stop the man from leaving the room, Tristan tried another angle.

"If you want power, you'll have to take it. Meliot will never let you be more than his lap dog, to sit and beg as he commands." When Ryan's shoulders sagged, Tristan knew the man believed him, already suspected as much.

"Meliot is very powerful; you made a mistake joining his ranks. There is only one way you'll ever leave this place. Believe me. I know."

A moan from the guard on the floor caught Ryan's attention. He kicked his downed cohort back to unconsciousness.

"This fuckin' sucks," Ryan yelled to no one in particular. The man stepped toward the table and Tristan waited to see what he would do. He placed his hands on Tristan's knees, sending healing power into the broken bones; the muscles around his knees tightened, accompanied by heat flowing through his legs.

"I wish I could do more for you." Ryan's tormented eyes met his before he stormed from the room.

THE FRIGID GROUND was hard when Gwen landed on her rear. Padraig stood next to her holding her hand. He pulled her up to her feet. "Sorry about that, it's hard to retain your balance when leaping." They were in an icy hell, nothing but white as far as she could see.

The alter-world was nothing like she expected. The air felt dense, the sky a strange hue of purple, with reddish streaks resembling claw marks across the expanse. There were trees, but they were not like any she'd ever seen. With twisted, blueish trunks, and ice-covered black leaves hanging from limbs that stretched sideways.

Big fluffy flakes fell to a ground already covered by grey-hued snow. Icy wind blew across the frozen expanse. She shivered, not only from the cold, but from fear of being stuck there forever.

In the distance, turrets of a castle caught her attention.

Just as Gwen was about to ask if it was where the evil wizard lived, the sound of a low, guttural growl announced the presence of an enormous white wolf. Gwen scurried behind Padraig and peeked around him at the wolf that stood silently watching them.

"Why is he staring at us like that? Is he hungry?" Gwen whispered. "I have a granola bar."

"No. He is a friend who guards the lands around Meliot's castle. Not unlike our home, which is surrounded by our enemies. It keeps balance in this world, I suppose." Padraig held his hand up to the wolf, in some sort of greeting gesture. Two additional wolves appeared, eyeing them with suspicion.

Seeming to be satisfied, like the humans had passed some sort of inspection, the wolves trotted away. Padraig took her hand. "They'll lead us to their leaders and shelter. The weather is about to get bad." He glanced at the sky. Gwen looked up as well, but didn't see anything that stood out.

She glanced back towards the castle. "I don't want to get shelter. We need to go rescue Tristan."

Padraig's eyes were soft. "I know. I can't stand the idea of him being there any longer." He hurried behind the wolves, Gwen almost jogging to keep up. "But we must let those that live here know why we're here, and hopefully they'll agree to help us. Just being invisible won't help us get Tristan out. If Niall was able to sense us, no doubt Meliot will too."

They arrived at a cave entrance. Two even larger wolves exited as they approached, and sat on their haunches watching their every move, but allowing them to enter.

Only the first wolf continued inside ahead of them. Gwen looked around in awe. The rock walls were smooth. Both sides flanked with lit torches every few feet. Once they arrived at a set of wooden doors, the large panels swung open slowly, allowing them into a large room, warmed by a huge fireplace.

On one side of the room, two women sat on tall throne-like chairs. Both turned to watch them enter, neither looking surprised. A wolf sat between them, no doubt the messenger.

Padraig walked a few paces in front of Gwen and fell to one knee in front of the women. He reverted to old English. "Greetings, Your Highnesses, I am Sir Padraig Clarre, knight to James the First, King of Scotland. The lady is Gwyneth Lockhart of America. We've come to seek your assistance in rescuing Laird Tristan McRainey, the Laird of *Dunimarle Castle*, subject of King James the First. He is being held prisoner by Meliot."

Gwen watched in fascination, as the women seemed to communicate telepathically, looking at each other, but not speaking. They wore long, richly colored, fur-trimmed robes. The women, who were either twins or sisters, had the same long platinum hair that matched the frozen world outside. They were not beautiful, but striking, with bright-blue eyes and flawless pearly skin, their faces unadorned with any makeup. One wore an emerald-green robe, while the other a ruby-red one. Neither wore a crown, but if they had, it wouldn't have surprised her. She noticed that Padraig had not risen, and she wondered if she should kneel as well. Or curtsy.

"Rise, Knight," The women in red spoke, her voice a thick velvety sound. "Welcome, Lady Gwyneth. Please sit." She motioned to two chairs with wide flat arms.

Once they sat, servants appeared and served them a hot beverage which looked like tea. The cups sat on the arms of the chairs along with a small tray of what looked to be shortbread. Padraig did not drink or eat, and Gwen followed suit. The women lifted their cups and took drinks. Only after they placed their cups down did Padraig lift his. Gwen drank from hers and was pleasantly surprised by the sweet flavor of the liquid. She didn't dare speak, so she thanked them with a smile.

The woman in green spoke. "I'm Esmeralda, this is my sister Rubiana. We are the Princesses of Atlandia, as this region is called. Our land borders Meliot's. The wizard is not a friendly neighbor." She glanced at her sister. "Our father left us to ensure that his power is not used against our people and to maintain control of our region, protect it against his evil."

Rubiana clapped her hands, and a large man walked in. The male wore a heavy woolen tunic, brown leather pants, and fur-lined boots. He was flanked by two wolves. "Argo, once the Icing passes, you are to escort our guests, Sir Padraig and Lady Lockhart, to the neighboring lands and assist in the rescue of their friend."

Argo, a large, powerfully built warrior, looked at them, acknowledging Padraig with a nod. He turned back to the princesses. "How many men should I take, Your Highnesses?"

"Six men and two wolves will go," Esmeralda replied.

Rubiana spoke next. "And Argo, ensure everyone returns."

Esmeralda turned to Padraig, eyes locked with his. "Ensure your ward of protection is strong enough to keep my men and sentries safe. They die only if you die with them."

His expression blank, Padraig replied without hesitation. "Understood. We are deeply grateful for your assistance."

Chapter Twenty-Four

The chamber she was given was spacious and warm. Pulling aside the draperies, Gwen looked out. Sleet continued falling, so thick she couldn't see anything. She shuddered and turned away, not envying anyone stuck outside in that. If it was a daily occurrence, how were they to avoid it after the rescue? Would they make it back to the caves in time?

She paced the room after discarding her jacket and knapsack on the bed. They'd told her the icing would last about four hours and she should rest. They'd leave as soon as it passed. As much as she agreed that rest was a good idea, she knew sleep would evade her.

Nightmares of Tristan hurting and calling for her would assail her if she tried. Nonetheless, there wasn't much she could do, and she'd need all her strength to remain invisible. Eyeing the bed, she considered lying down anyway.

A rap at the door startled her, and she called for the

person to enter. It was Padraig. The knight walked in. He'd also removed his heavy winter furs. "There is one thing we need to discuss before leaving." He motioned for her to sit and joined her. "Tristan may not be able to walk out. I will have to carry him." He hesitated. "My loyalty is to Tristan, but as a knight I am sworn to protect those who are threatened and cannot defend themselves. Please don't make me choose, because I will have to do the honorable thing. You are a lady."

"It would be more honorable to rescue Tristan rather than me, Padraig." She reached for his hand and squeezed. "In this case he is more vulnerable that I am. If for some reason I don't return, please ensure that my sister frees Tristan. Don't let this all be for nothing."

Padraig didn't look convinced. "I assure you Tristan will not forgive me if I were to leave you behind, if a choice is to be made. Perhaps you should stay here and await our return."

"No!" Gwen cried. "I'm going! You said yourself, you are not strong enough to do this alone. We must combine our strengths to be able to stand against Meliot. Now, let's not waste any more time talking. Show me how we can combine our power. I need to know how to shoot energy and flatten some wizard ass."

THEY TREKKED over the frozen terrain by foot. There was no way to tell time, but to Gwen it seemed as if at least two hours had past when it began snowing again. Why didn't they use horses? Or make sleds and train the huge wolves to pull them, like the Eskimos did? That would make more sense than the slow process of walking, no stumbling, to the enemy.

She glanced at Padraig stern face. "Why don't you just flash us there?"

"It would be sensed by Meliot. Any simple ward would pick it up, same with horses or any other form of transportation. We'll be there shortly. The trip back will be faster, we can leap without care; they'll be more than aware of our presence by then."

Gwen concentrated on a snowdrift; lifting her hand she practiced sending an energy pulse to it. The snowbank burst, sending flurries into the air. She grinned like a fool until a wolf looked back and growled at her. "Just practicing," Gwen told it. The wolf turned away.

Argo and another warrior walked in front of her and Padraig, behind them another four. One wolf remained beside Argo. The other wolf went ahead of them as soon as they left the caves.

Argo held his hand up signaling for them to stop. Gwen sent Padraig a questioning look. He shrugged in response. They waited for a few moments, until the wolf who'd been ahead of them returned. He went straight to Argo and sat. The warrior seemed to be communicating with the wolf, and then spoke to the group.

"The gate has four guards. Two are human, the other two are not. Inside the gate there are two sentries. The wolves will take care of the sentries.

"Once inside the gates, your wards will have to keep us from being seen from the watchmen. There is one watchman at each of the four turrets. We won't bother with them, but they are archers, so if they spot us, it will be problematic."

You think?

The warrior motioned at four men. "Go in behind us. We will see to the front guards and sentries. Go straight to the front door. Do not wait to see the outcome of our fight—take them in." He nodded toward Padraig and Gwen.

"Once inside, remain hidden until they return."

The men grumbled, disappointed to learn they were not expected to fight. Argo gave them a bland look. "If at any point they are discovered, you can kill anyone that stands in the way, anyone that tries to prevent them leaving the grounds." The men then became animated.

Gwen shook her head. Men—who could ever understand them?

When they finally got close enough to the castle to see the front gate, Gwen was shocked by the lack of protection. The guards at the gate sat inside a small guard shack, playing a sort of dice game. The gates were open. Meliot didn't seem to feel threatened. Argo and one of his men went into the guardhouse and quickly dispatched the unaware men.

Gwen turned her head away, concentrating on casting the wards for the group. She and Padraig were able to pass through the gate undetected. The wolves raced past them into the grounds. If the wolves were challenged by Meliot's sentinels, the fight was silent.

Gwen looked about nervously. When she stepped on a branch, and it cracked under her boot she sucked in a harsh breath. Nerves were getting the best of her. Glancing down, she noticed they were leaving footprints. Fortunately the falling snow covered them with swiftness.

They arrived at the front doors of the castle. Another set of guards stood flanking the doorway. Unlike the gate guards, these men were watchful. Argo's men approached silently. Both guards were grabbed from behind and dragged away with barely a struggle. The warriors opened the front door and stepped inside, one of them motioning for Gwen and Padraig to follow.

The front rooms were eerily empty. Argo's men must have hidden upon entering, because Gwen did not see anyone. "Now." Padraig disappeared, and she followed suit.

"This way," he whispered, taking her hand.

They went down a long corridor, when two of Meliot's men walked towards them. Gwen flattened herself against the wall, her heart beating so fast she was sure it was audible. She held her breath until they walked past, and only when Padraig tugged her hand did she remember to breathe again.

Coming to a door, they hesitated again. "We'll have to wait." Padraig spoke right into her ear. She wondered how he knew where her ear was. Was she not invisible enough? He must have sensed her tenseness. "I can see the outline of your aura," Padraig explained.

She nodded, afraid to speak. The door's hinges creaked as they opened, and a man stormed out. He didn't bother closing the door behind him. Padraig and Gwen rushed in. They hurried down a stairway.

The room was dark and smelled of blood and other bodily fluids. A man lay unconscious or dead on the floor, next to a wooden slab on which Tristan lay. A gasp escaped her at the sight of the myriads of injuries on Tristan's body. Chained by his wrists and ankles, he was on his back. Seeming awake, eyes open, he stared at the ceiling. His hair was matted, and she could see dried blood all over him. Large, angry bruises covered his torso and legs. His knees were purple, and his jaw and both eyes swollen almost shut. Needing to comfort him, she started to move toward him, but Padraig pulled her back.

"Unlock the chains. I will go and speak into his ear, so he will not fight when I pick him up. He is going to be invisible. I will be carrying him. Once he disappears, begin the protection ward I taught you. I cannot carry him, keep our wards up, and also help you, so do your best."

His hand dropped hers and Gwen concentrated on the chains. She glanced up when Tristan turned his head to the side. Padraig must have spoken because his eyes scanned the room. She forced herself to ignore him as one by one the cuffs fell open.

"Gwen, please go," Tristan rasped, his eyes wildly scouring the room. Then he was gone. Gwen turned and ran out of the room.

Desperation and fear were the ultimate motivators, running up the stairs and down the first corridor, she could think of nothing more than escaping. Thoughts of anything other than breaking out into the frozen grounds guided her as she flew past a doorway and finally reached the front room.

Before she could reach the front door, it slammed shut. Meliot's guards flanking it, other guard's swords began slicing the air. Unsure of what to do, she went to the nearest wall and pressed against it.

The man who'd stormed out of the room Tristan was held in earlier ran into the room. "Where is his lordship? The prisoner escaped."

A cloud of smoke swirled then spread, dissipating slowly, showing an older man who stood at the high board, his eyes blazing. "Find him now," he screamed. He turned to a new set of guards just entering. "There are others in the room—find them."

The wizard narrowed his eyes and glanced in her direction. Gwen closed her eyes concentrating on her spell to block him from seeing her. It seemed to work.

Meliot emanated evil. She'd never doubt again that such darkness existed. Black power oozed from the wizard, but she was surprised by its lackluster. He seemed to rely on his men to do all the dirty work. Two men stood beside him and began throwing energy bursts into the room.

She cringed and slid down to the floor fast and crawled toward the door.

An explosion sounded and the heavy doors were flung open. Two white wolves rushed the guards. She gasped in surprise when the princesses' warriors appeared within the room, their swords drawn.

Argo and another warrior also ran in from outside. They went straight toward Meliot. Anticipating them, the wizard raised his hand and flames lashed at the men, who held up shields and continued moving toward him.

The wards were holding.

The fighting was swift. The princesses' men were well

trained with the sword. Even to her untrained eyes, it was evident that Meliot's guardsmen were in trouble. Their responses slow, their attacks easily blocked.

It was difficult going, trying to get to the front door while avoiding the feuding men and flying swords. She prayed that Padraig had made it out with Tristan. Finally, seeing an opening, she hurried through it to the open doorway and ran out into the cold. She stumbled past the guard shack to their agreed-upon meeting place. The snow was falling heavily now, making it hard to see.

Exhausted from holding the wards up, she walked as fast as she could into the woods, following the path Argo marked earlier. A white wolf came alongside her. Gwen felt an uneasy comfort at his presence. The wolf quietly walked beside her until they reached their designated spot. Finally feeling somewhat safe, Gwen went to a fallen tree and collapsed on it, the wolf sitting on its haunches in front of her.

Crying would be easy, but she feared the moistness from her tears would freeze onto her face. Wrapping her arms around her, she rocked back and forth, anxious to hear an approach. After a few minutes, she gave up hope. In all probability, Padraig had taken Tristan back to their home and was too weak to come and find her.

She eyed the wolf who remained on his haunches. "Can you take me back to the palace?"

The creature turned to look at her and then up to the sky. Then to her surprise, he nudged her leg until she lowered to sit again, wrapping her useless cloak around herself.

"You're right. If they survived, they've gone to find shelter."

The wolf moved closer, lay against her, and lowered its huge head to cover her as much as possible.

"This is the one time I am not going to complain about personal space," Gwen said, shivering despite the wolf's attempts to keep her warm.

To her horror, The Icing began.

Chapter Twenty-Five

Vibrations shook the ground. Hooves? Horses maybe? Gwen tried to sit up, but her body was too heavy. A frigid blanket of snow covered her. Her eyelids weighty, she wanted nothing more than to sleep. Strange that she felt numb both physically and mentally, the only thoughts were hopes that Tristan was safe. Sleet continued falling, heavy ice pellets pounding through her blanket of snow.

Something nudged her shoulder. Forcing her eyes open was difficult, but she managed to crack them open. The wolf shifted. The rumbling became louder, whatever caused it coming closer.

Large white and grey wolves broke through the trees; one picked her up and threw her across his wide back, barely breaking his stride. They were being chased, the pursuers snarling loudly. More wolves?

Bouncing on the wolf's back, her limbs heavy and too tired to try to do much more than hang limply across his back, Gwen wondered if she would survive. The ice painfully pelted her as they raced through the woods.

Moments later, the warmth of the wolf began seeping into her and she reveled in it. Opening her eyes, she could see the ground whizzing past. Amazed she didn't fall off, she turned and got a glimpse of their pursuers. Black wolves, barely visible through the falling sleet.

Finally they slowed. The pursuers no longer chased them. Their eerie howls echoed into the forest. No doubt, a promise of revenge.

Arriving in a dense portion of the forest, the sleet didn't fall as hard. The wolf that carried her crouched down and another picked her up off his back, his teeth grabbing the back of her jacket. She was placed on the ground with surprising gentleness. Too weak to get up, she waited to find out her fate.

Six of the wolves began to convulse. Howls and snarling pounding in her ears, she covered them, curling into a ball. The wolves transformed into Argo and his men. The warriors stood, fully nude. As if waking from a long sleep, they stretched and shook their heads.

They were werewolves.

"You're werewolves." Laughter escaped her, an insane sound.

"Shifters," Argo replied.

"Naked men, in the middle of a blizzard. Why not?" She laughed harder, rolling over holding her stomach. As she wiped away tears from the hysterical laughter, she pointed at the two wolves that remained. "Are they stuck?"

Argo cocked his head, frowning at her. "No, they are

sentinels, their basic form is as wolves, but they can shift to human."

"Well, now that we're clear." She began to laugh again, the laughter merging into sobs.

Someone picked her up and they hurried back into the Icing.

"Did Padraig and Tristan get away?" She met Argo's eyes, hoping to see the truth.

The man shook his head. "I do not know. It is possible."

Not reassuring in the least.

Gwen remained in the Atlandia Princesses' guest room for two days. Sleeping most of the time, tucked under heavy furs, she woke only to eat, then fell back into a deep slumber.

On the third day, she woke feeling completely recovered. Dashing from the bed, she made her way to the throne room. Only Esmeralda was present, sitting at a table, parchment unfolded in front of her. The princess's bright eyes met hers, then she smiled. "I am glad to see you. Have you recovered fully? We were worried."

"Yes, I feel well enough to travel. Thank you so much. I truly am in your debt. I need to go to the knights' keep immediately. Please." The last word cracked, her need to see Tristan immense.

"Argo and his men will escort you as soon as the Icing passes." The princess's eyes were kind when she motioned for Gwen to come and sit near her.

"We are not able to leap as they are. Unfortunately, the only one that can do it is our brother Sterling, who does not reside here. He prefers to roam Atlandia, pursuing other matters."

From the way the princess curled her lip on the last word, Gwen gathered they were on the outs with Prince Sterling.

"Horseback is fine. Or however you travel," she said, hoping she didn't have to ride across a wolf's back again

"Aye, we travel by horse or by carriage, although carriages can be cumbersome in the woods as there are few roads."

THEY LEFT THE FOLLOWING DAY, Argo and two others escorting her back to the knights' keep on horseback. It took almost eight hours. Once they'd arrived on the knights' lands, Padraig and Liam appeared and guided them to their home. Meliot's horsemen no longer surrounded the keep.

She hurried inside ahead of them, into the quiet great room. As Argo's men entered behind her, the men greeted each other. The shifters were invited to stay the night. They'd leave in the morning to avoid the Icing.

Gwen pulled Padraig aside. "Where is Tristan? Can I see him?"

Uneasiness was quickly covered up. "He is here, upstairs in his chamber. Niall is with him. He has not quite recovered as yet." Gwen began to move toward the stairs. Padraig stopped her, his hand catching her elbow.

"I'm sorry, Gwyneth. He doesn't want to see you."

Her widened eyes flew to his face. "What? Why not?"

"He's been through a lot. It's discomforting for a man to be seen in such a vulnerable state. Give him a couple of days."

She sank into a chair and stared blankly into the fireplace. Had Tristan specifically told them he didn't want to see her? She'd come so far to save him, and this was the result? Two days she'd been stuck recovering. It was a long time here in the alter-world. They didn't have the luxury of indefinite time.

"He and I need to begin working the spell," Gwen murmured. "There is much to do."

Padraig nodded. "I know."

"Would you like some tea?" Liam neared and held out a steaming cup to her. "You must be hungry. I'll get food."

Gwen took the cup, but didn't drink from it.

Dinner was a somber event. They ate from large wooden platters full of meat and what looked like boiled potatoes. The shifters ate only the meat. Gwen had her fill, more than she expected.

"I need to speak to Tristan. It is ridiculous to give in to his sense of male pride at a time like this."

Liam frown. "He is being healed. Needs to conserve his strength."

"And I can help," Gwen insisted.

When a visibly pale Niall came down the stairs and sat at the table, he acknowledged the visitors before looking toward her. "I am glad to see you are well."

He piled his plate with food and began eating. His hand shook as he drank from his cup. No one asked him any questions, allowing him to eat in peace.

The shifters finished eating and left to check on their

horses before bunking in the great room for the night, where pallets were already set out for them. Liam, the perfect host, began adding wood to the fire in the large fireplace.

"How is he?" Gwen asked Niall, who glanced at Padraig before answering. "His injuries are healing." The curt reply did not satisfy her.

"I'll take his dinner up," Liam said, grabbing a plate piled with food.

Uneasiness filled the room.

"Tell me the truth," Gwen snapped. "What is going on? Something is wrong with Tristan. What is it?"

Gavin cleared his throat, his amber eyes looking around the table before meeting hers. "You are correct, something happened to him. We've tried to talk to him, but he refuses to budge."

"Budge? About what?"

"Tristan does not wish to be freed any longer. He insists you be returned. He is choosing to remain here, in the alter-world."

"*Tristan does not wish to be freed any longer.*" Later that night, Gwen sat on the bed, the words repeating in her head.

"The hell with this," she muttered. If Tristan didn't want to see her, too bad. He'd just have to deal with it. She'd confront him and find out the truth.

The hallway was empty as she made her way toward Tristan's room. She stopped hearing the men inside in a heated conversation.

"You're deciding all our fates based on something Meliot showed you!" Padraig shouted. "What the fuck did he do that would make you decide to keep us all here?"

Liam spoke now. "You are aware the wizard will use any and all manners of deception to keep us here, aren't you? If you tell us what he said, or showed you, we can help."

"Our entire existence is an illusion, the enchantment, nothing is real. What does it matter?" Gavin's voice was full of bitterness, he seemed to be on Tristan's side. "Let's just resign ourselves to the truth. We'll never leave."

"At least tell us the reason our fate is sealed." Padraig asked.

Gwen slid down to the floor. She'd learn more by remaining out of the room right now.

TRISTAN'S entire world was upside down. He hated everything at this moment. Hated the faces of his best friends that registered everything from panic to sadness. He hated himself most of all.

He'd brought this upon them. From that fateful day when he'd summoned them to go with him to meet with the council of knights.

The years of imprisonment, losing their families, their entire lives. It was all his fault.

Gwen remained in the keep. He sensed her presence.

How he wished to find comfort with her right now. Needed her more than ever but didn't deserve to be comforted. He deserved nothing but the stabs of pain shooting through him when looking at the men who'd been through so much, and revealing to them that they were never leaving.

Flashbacks of the torture assailed him, and he fell back, covering his face. When the shaking began, he tried to force it away. It only got worse.

"Leave!" he yelled past chattering teeth. "Go and leave me be."

"It will pass." Liam spoke from experience. No one left the room.

Niall came to him and placing his hands on his shoulders. Heat engulfed Tristan and he gulped air, trying to stabilize. Niall had to be weak by now.

Regaining some semblance of normalcy, he pushed Niall's hands away gently, owing the Scot a great deal.

"Thank you," he told Niall, "I don't deserve your help. You are right, Paddy. You deserve to know." Tristan took a deep breath.

"Meliot has my daughter. He will never release her if I leave."

"It has to be an illusion," Padraig yelled. "Don't fall for his tricks, Tristan."

"If he'd held her prisoner for this long, he would have used her against you before now," Liam said.

Tristan let out a weary sigh. "It has to be true. Clara disappeared right after our enchantment began. I heard talk about it in the house." Tristan shook with anger. "I was nae aware of having a daughter until after the enchantment.

There was talk about it. My family sent out men who searched for her for days without success."

The men remained silent seeming unsure how to respond.

"I have a recurring dream she's being chased through the woods. I don't see who or what chases her. It always ends the same, with her scream of terror. I've always suspected Meliot's involvement in her disappearance." He leaned over and rubbed his hands over his face. "I cannot imagine what she has gone through all these years."

The men were silent. Padraig shook his head. "I don't know what it's like to have a child, but I understand why you are reluctant to test him in this. I pledged my fidelity to you from the beginning. I agree to remain. If she is there, we must find her and free her."

Niall glanced around the room, meeting each of their gazes. "Are all in agreement that we will stay?"

Everyone nodded and replied together. "Aye."

"It's decided then," Niall told them. "We stay."

"I'll take Gwyneth back," Gavin told them.

Gwen burst into the room. Ignoring the other men, she went straight to Tristan and planted herself in front of him, hands on her hips. "This is bullshit and you know it. We haven't come this far only for you to allow that wizard to trip you up with a trick. Because that is all this is." She glared at him, not allowing the agony in his eyes to affect her. "I had the same dream not that long ago. Don't you see, it's one of his many ways to get you to stop trying."

"You cannot possibly understand." Tristan covered his face with both hands and rolled to his side. The defeated posture tore through her. She placed her hand on his shoulder.

"Tristan, I do understand. I have sisters that I love more than life. But at the same time, you have to know that Meliot is probably lying."

The others left to give them privacy, Gwen kept trying to dissuade Tristan out of giving up until he finally fell into an exhausted sleep.

Niall returned, went to the bed and placed his hands over him. Gwen watched, fascinated as light came from his palms and radiated into Tristan's body. Other than moaning, he didn't wake up.

"He's badly injured, but he will want to be healed so that we can go and rescue his daughter," Niall told her, his grey eyes meeting hers. "Gavin will take you back to your world as soon as you are ready."

"I won't be until morning," Gwen replied. Expecting an argument, she continued. "Just give me a few hours. I'm trying to figure this out. I don't know that I can leave you guys here, trapped forever."

"What proof did Meliot give? I refuse to believe it is true?"

. "None that I heard." The large Irishman glanced at the bed. "Were ye willing to carry out the sacrifice?"

"I was never told what it was." Gwen's mind spun. "Tristan said he wasn't clear on what it is. I haven't had the opportunity to consider it."

He shrugged, "It doesna matter now. Our fate is sealed."

She reached and placed her hand on his forearm. His eyes widened, his entire body tensing. She snatched her hand back. Bad idea. The man had not been touched by a woman in centuries. "How can you give up so easily? Niall, talk him out of it. He seems to listen to you."

"He will not change his mind. We can't keep you here verra much longer." He gave her a crooked smile, melting her heart, and without thinking, she stood on her toes and kissed him on the cheek. Hearing his intake of breath, she moved away.

"Thank you, Niall. For everything you are doing for him."

Chapter Twenty-Six

This was a very bad idea. Probably the worst idea she'd ever had. Gwen stumbled, falling for the third time. It was pitch-black outside. She couldn't even see her hand in front of her face. With arms outstretched, she continued forward, away from the keep.

She began to chant the spell warding herself from being seen and sensed. Perhaps if she built a bubble, she could avoid trees or worse, cliffs. She ran into a tree limb and yelped in pain. So much for that idea.

She'd remained in Tristan's room for hours, chanting the freeing spell over the sleeping Tristan, again and again. While chanting, her sacrifice became clear. Suddenly she knew what the sacrifice was, and it tore her entire being to shreds.

Was she willing to sacrifice everything to save a man? Leave the life she knew forever and risk losing her own life?

Four men had been living here, in this utterly horrible place, for hundreds of years. They'd been toyed with and tortured, held in limbo with no hope.

Picturing her sisters, tears trickled down her face. Sabrina and Tabitha would understand, but they would be heartbroken.

Her mind was made up. If she had to remain here and take Tristan's place, she would do it.

Whether or not Clara was here, was not clear. In truth, Gwen doubted the child had been held here, but she would find out.

The decision part was easy, but now outside in the darkness, she began to have second thoughts. Perhaps she should have formulated a better plan. Something more than just getting out of the keep undetected and running away, in hopes Meliot's minions would find her and take her back to his castle.

When she was snatched up and carried away, she felt almost relieved. Whatever carried her didn't seem to be affected by her ward spell. Flying up into the air, Gwen suppressed a scream. Whatever the creature, it was surprisingly gentle in the way it held her in his huge claws. The sound of its wings flapping and the wind whooshing past let her know they moved at a very fast speed.

After what seemed like an hour, she saw lights.

Meliot's castle was ahead. Her plan had worked.

The dragon—she could see the animal now—landed in a clearing and deposited her, again with surprising gentleness. He stood beside her, as if waiting for someone to approach. She stole a glance at the dragon. Its red eyes scanned the area, looking for movement. If she didn't know any better, she'd swear the huge beast protected her. However, if he killed anyone that tried to come near her, she wouldn't be able to meet with Meliot.

"I need to go to the castle. Can you help me?" Gwen asked the dragon. His intelligent eyes met hers, but he didn't budge.

She chanted the spell to break Tristan free again, just to be safe. Then she turned back to the beast. "Can you take me to Meliot?" He crouched down, placing his head on the ground, his eyes closed. Gwen took a step away and his eyes flashed open. She held her hands up. "Okay, not moving."

Black wolves moved in the distance. They circled but didn't come near. She wondered if these were shifters or just sentinels. The dragon lifted his head and growled. The wolves shifted nervously, but didn't leave.

Gwen turned to the dragon; he studied the wolves, ignoring her. "I need to go to that castle." She pointed toward the building. "Either take me over there or let me go on my own."

"There are better methods to kill oneself." A beautiful man walked towards the dragon and her. "I believe your magic cannot best Meliot's."

Tall, dark, and handsome, he was the personification of a fairy-tale prince. He walked to the dragon and stroked his head. "Well done."

"I need to speak to Meliot. Can you think of a better way?" She studied him. "Who are you?"

"I am Sterling. This is Caspian." He motioned to the dragon. "He must have sensed your distress and went to find you." Sterling's cerulean-blue eyes searched her face. "Are you the enchantress who visited my sisters?"

Gwen couldn't believe her luck. Of all times for a prince to come to her rescue, he came when she didn't want it. She bit back the urge to laugh.

The resemblance to his sisters became obvious. His almost chestnut-brown, shoulder-length hair, his brilliant blue eyes and the same pale, perfect complexion were identical to Esmeralda and Rubiana's. Unlike his sisters, Sterling dressed in modern attire, thick leather jacket, jeans, and biker boots.

He looked toward the castle and shook his head. "You can summon him, but I wouldn't go any nearer. The sentinels don't exactly stop and ask your purpose for visiting before tearing limb from limb."

Gwen grimaced at the thought and glanced to the wolves. "How do I summon him?" She asked, getting aggravated, wanting to get this confrontation over with before losing her nerve.

The prince stuck out his hand. A black amulet hung from it. "Take this. Wait until I leave, then call him." He gave her a long look. "Are you sure?"

Gwen nodded. "Yes."

"It is a mistake. You cannot trust him. But it is your decision." Sterling patted the dragon's head, and it pushed itself upright, spreading its wings and flying away gracefully. He whistled, and a large white horse came out of the trees. *Of course.*

"The best defense is the truth." Sterling said, and with that he jumped into the saddle and turned to leave.

"Hey, Charming?" Gwen called. When he turned, she waved. "Thank you."

"It's Sterling, and again I advise against what you are about to do." He rode away, not looking back.

"Crap." Gwen stared at the amulet. *Am I really doing this?* "Meliot!" She shouted, "I need to talk to you."

Nothing happened. So she tried again.

This time there was a soft rustle of wind, followed by a dark puff of smoke, and the wizard appeared. Once again, she was taken aback by the malevolence that emanated from him.

"I don't like to be summoned," he told her, his black eyes narrowing at the amulet hanging from her hand. "Give that to me."

"I don't think so," Gwen replied, pulling it on over her head. "It's not mine to give away."

She tried to appear nonchalant as fear gripped her. Her nails bit into her fisted palms, clenched tight to keep from shaking. "I came to complete the last part of the freeing spell and break the enchantment. The sacrificial portion is mine, I believe."

The wizard's eyes widened. He actually looked surprised. "You can't possibly be serious. You have no idea what you are doing, paltry witch."

Pacing before her, it was obvious he was considering a way to thwart her plans.

"You have to accept it, Meliot. You made the rules. You can't break them. Unless what they say about you is true." His head snapped to her, eyes narrowed. "That you never keep your word, that when bested you devise another hurdle to be passed."

"I am not above reproach, however I've yet to be bested," he retorted angrily, spittle flying from his lips. Good, she'd struck a nerve. "Do you have any idea what will be asked of you?" His eyes gleamed, his lips curved into a smile giving her chills.

"Yes, I do."

"I am here to take Clara's place."

Chapter Twenty-Seven

Thunderstorms reminded him of another lifetime, another life altogether. The sounds of rain, followed by thunder soothed him. Tristan lay in bed listening to the symphony played by nature. Life was easy here in the alter-world, he admitted. No choices, pretty much just an existence of living day-to-day.

How had he allowed himself to sleep for so long! He got up from the bed, ignoring the pains that remained, and began getting dressed.

Gwyneth was gone, probably already taken back to the other realm. He didn't feel the now familiar pull to follow, to join her in her world. Perhaps now that he'd given up on the idea of leaving, everything stopped.

His chest tightened and he fought to keep his composure. After so long, he'd finally felt hope and love. Gwen was everything he could have ever hoped for. And now, she was gone. Tristan pushed the heels of his hands into his eyes.

He wanted to rage, to scream,, to break things, but didn't have the luxury. Instead he sat down to pull on his boots.

Gavin walked in. Tristan didn't have to look to know. The man was like a disoriented bear. The bang of his boot against the door as he walked in left no doubt. The large knight sat down, his golden eyes peering at Tristan's face. "I figured ye would be awake by now?"

"If it is about Gwyneth, I do not want to talk about it."

"I understand your decision not to leave. None of us begrudge you that. I've been thinking..."

"We've all been thinking, Campbell."

"It is about yer daughter. Did you sense her presence?"

Tristan closed his eyes, his jaw tightening, recalling his time at Meliot's castle. It did not surprise him that after he'd damned these men to remain in the alter-world, they wanted to come up with a plan to help him.

"I didn't sense anything. The wizard promised to return her, after Gwyneth departed. He will send a messenger."

"Ah. But do we trust that?"

"Not one bit."

A wave of dizziness swept over Tristan, and he closed his eyes. "Is the room spinning?"

The rotating subsided, and he opened his eyes. Gavin stood over him a puzzled look on his face. "You were fading. Do you feel a pull to the other side?"

"No." He sat up, trying to get his bearings. "This time it was different. It is probably part of Niall's healing. I expected to feel compelled to follow her, but it has not happened."

"Or maybe, it is because she is still here, in this realm."

"What? Where is Gwyneth?" His hands fisted on the man's shirt. "What did she do?"

"She went to Meliot."

"No! Why did you not tell me?"

"You told me not to speak of her." Gavin replied, pulling Tristan's hands off his shirtfront. "You are fading again."

The spinning began again. This time, the room spun faster and faster, until Tristan feared he'd lose the entire contents of his stomach. Pitching back and forth, followed by the familiar rush of moving into another realm, he was gone. Darkness filled with stars swirled around him. He tried to grab onto something, but his hands came up empty. When he landed, he began heaving and gulping for air, trying his best not to throw up. There was no pain this time, only nausea.

Looking around, he fell back onto his back in shock. He was back at McRainey estates.

Only this time, he lay outside the keep.

"No!" He yelled into the night. "No, no, no!" He pounded his fists into the ground.

The enchantment had been broken. He was free.

A star shot across the night sky; he followed it until it disappeared. This wasn't right! He'd chosen to stay.

He wasn't sure how long he lay on the ground trying to convince himself to get up, but remained frozen, fearful. The stark realization that once he got up and went into the keep, he'd have to begin his new life, kept him from moving.

Almost four hundred years later and he was finally free.

How could he want a life at the cost of losing his daughter again?

Gwyneth, she'd sacrificed herself, and as expected, Meliot reneged. "Let her go," Tristan yelled into the night. "Take me back." A tear rolled down the side of his face to the ground, he wiped it away angrily and sat up. Meliot would not release them. Not willingly.

"This is not ending like this, Meliot. You will not win."

Finally he stood and shakily walked toward the keep.

THE FRONT DOOR WAS UNLOCKED. Tristan found it surprising that he was able to enter and acclimate himself to the first floor of the house without anyone stumbling upon him. How long he had waited for this moment, the day he'd walk in this house freely, without being confined to the room he flashed into.

Footsteps came to a halt, and he turned to see Edith McRainey. After an initial shocked look, she rushed to him, hugging him. "You're free. Thank God and the Virgin Mary!" Edith exclaimed. "Oh goodness, I can barely believe it." The older woman began to cry, reaching up and cupping his face. "You've been through so much. I know you'll need some time to adjust." She looked around him. "Where's Gwen?"

"Meliot took Gwyneth. I have to go back."

"What?" Edith cried, "Oh no. What am I going to tell her sister?"

"Don't worry Edith, I overheard." A young woman walked into the room, her eyes trained on Tristan. It had to be Gwyneth's sister. Their resemblance was uncanny, in spite of their very different coloring. Where Gwyneth was dark, this sister was fair. In contrast to Gwen's midnight hair, her hair was vibrant in different shades of red and auburn that framed her pretty face. Her eyes were light, not dark brown like Gwen's, but they both had the same almond shape.

"I'm Sabrina." She held her hand out. Tristan took it. "Is this the last part of the enchantment? The sacrifice. Since the other parts are done."

"Done?" Tristan asked confused.

"Yes, you know, the correct spell and the part where the enchantress falls in love with you," Sabrina told him holding his gaze. "You are aware that now you'll have to marry her, right?"

He knew his eyes widened, but he hoped she didn't take it the wrong way. "She's in love with me?"

Sabrina cocked an eyebrow. "Duh."

"Of course I'll do my duty by her," he stuttered.

"Your *duty*? You'll only marry her if you love her. Not out of duty. Men! No matter what time you're from, you guys are all the same. Dense."

"Should not we be worrying about saving her first?"

"On it." She held up her hand. "I'm going to look for a spell in the book, but I'm almost certain it's not necessary." She gave him a triumphant look. "The enchantment is broken. She can't possibly stay there now."

Tristan wasn't too sure, but he didn't argue. He needed time to think. Perhaps he'd summon Gavin and get him to flash him back to the alter-world.

"What the hell is going on?" The young McRainey entered the room, stopping, his mouth falling open when he set eyes on Tristan. "Oh."

"Nephew," Tristan greeted him, not moving, afraid he might hit the man for touching Gwyneth. "Unlike the ladies, you do not seem pleased at my return."

Derrick's eyes narrowed slightly. He went to pour himself a drink and drank it down, then poured another.

"It's just that I didn't think the legend was true," he told them without turning. "How the hell could this happen?"

When he turned, his expression was completely composed. "Welcome back, Laird. I'm pleased that you are free and can finally return to your home."

Tristan nodded, watching the young man pour another drink, then pour one in a separate glass and bring it to him. "How long since you've been able to—partake?" The question was not about the drink... Tristan understood that.

"Just a few days ago, actually," Tristan replied, locking gazes with Derrick's. "I enjoyed it very much."

"I find that hard to believe," Derrick replied, also not backing off. "If so, you would not be so eager to leave this alter-world."

"I didn't say it happened there," Tristan replied, lifting an eyebrow and glancing toward the ceiling. "Did I?"

Derrick stared at him, not breaking eye contact as he took another swallow from his glass.

Sabrina huffed. "If this testosterone standoff is done, we need to concentrate on saving my sister."

Chapter Twenty-Eight

In the tension-filled room, Tristan stared blankly at the fireplace. He was home. He never expected it to come to pass. For hundreds of years, it was always an inaccessible dream. Now, he was finally free and couldn't be happy that the dream finally came true. Not this way. Instead of being relieved, other emotions battled within him—loneliness, confusion, and fear. He hated admitting the last one. He feared the consequences of Gwyneth's actions. He couldn't even begin to fathom what Meliot would do to her. If so, he'd go crazy with rage.

Meliot had to be killed.

"I'll go check on dinner. You must be starved," Edith said, her brows drawn together.

"Thank you," Tristan replied, noting that Derrick watched him intently, as if in deep thought.

"I understand how you feel," he told the young McRainey. "I was two-and-thirty when I was given three days to prepare to leave everything I knew behind. I, too, thought my future was set. I was betrothed, about to become the Laird of the clan."

Derrick listened without replying, unmoving, his lips pressed in a straight line.

Tristan continued. "The hardest part of the enchantment was turning over leadership to my younger brother. Although he'd be a fair and good laird, it didn't soften the blow. I was turning over to someone else everything that I'd waited for, my entire life. He even married the woman I was to marry."

He'd never shared all of this with anyone, but now that he'd begun, he couldn't stop. "For many years I was angry, in a rage over the unfairness of my destiny. I did not care about anything or anyone for a long time. When I was able to come here to the estate, I saw the changes, the people, children. Everything that had been taken from me. Seeing all the changes only enraged me more. I did not begrudge them, that they had the life I was meant to have—at least that's what I told myself. But I did. In truth, I hated them, hated the normalcy of their lives."

"I'm sorry," Derrick finally replied. The young man seemed sincere. "I can't imagine what you went through. The loss of my plans seems insignificant in comparison."

"They are not. You thought your future was set. I won't give up my home now that I've regained it. I'm not even sure what the cost of it is, as of yet. If I have lost my daughter, and if Gwyneth sacrificed herself for me to be here, I cannot turn it over to you." He had an afterthought. "Where do you live?"

"I live in one of many McRainey homes. My home is not

very far from here. It is younger than this estate, built in the 1800s. Not as large either. The lands and home are about half the size. You'll have to come and see it soon."

"It will be my pleasure," Tristan said.

The young McRainey seemed to relax. Tristan wondered if he would be as accommodating once it all sank in.

Edith returned, Sabrina with her. The women announced dinner, and they stood to join them. Throughout the meal, Sabrina eyed him, biting her bottom lip in thought. The expression reminded him of Gwen, and he looked down at his plate.

"My sister told me that during those three days prior to the enchantment, many enchantresses and wizards visited each of you, to try to help. Did any of them mention an arbitrator? Is there someone besides Meliot with the power to oversee the breaking of the enchantment?"

Tristan mulled it over. "In the alter-world, there are three guardians, two Princesses and a Prince, who seem to keep Meliot under control. For the most part they concentrate on their lands and people's safety. They have never interceded for us. If we request an audience and ask for their help, they have been supportive, and aided in the way of guidance or additional warriors. They have a small army of wolf-shifters and sentinels."

"Do you think they will help rescue Gwen if she needs it?"

"I've already considered that. Upon my arrival here, I called for Gavin to come. My summons has gone unanswered. Perhaps you can try."

Sabrina was pensive, "I will try. When Campbell came for

Gwen, he told us that her magic would be much stronger in the alter-world. Are you aware of that? Is it strong enough for her to stand against Meliot?"

"Yes, it is stronger, although not stronger than Meliot's. Padraig reported she was able to maintain their invisibility and kept us from being sensed by Meliot and his minions. I am counting on that to keep her safe."

"I hate to bring this up right now, but it's necessary," Edith said, her gentle eyes meeting his. "We must send for the city council; they have to be made aware of your return. Also, we must notify the family. We'll have to call for the entire McRainey clan." She turned to Derrick next. "He needs clothes. Can you pick up some things, dear?"

"Of course, Aunt Edith." Derrick looked at Tristan. "I'll need to measure you—I'm not sure what to call you; you look too young for *Grandfather*."

The moment of levity was needed. "Just *Tristan* is fine," he replied. "I agree, Edith. As soon as I am properly dressed, we can meet with the city council. A couple of days maybe?" She nodded in agreement.

"They could request DNA testing," Derrick said, "Those results will be interesting. He's probably pure McRainey."

Tristan had no idea what Derrick spoke about. He returned his attention to Sabrina. "Did you find anything in your book that will help? Can we try to summon Gavin now?" He was anxious to get Gwen out of Meliot's clutches.

Two hours later, Derrick had left. Edith excused herself to allow Sabrina and Tristan time to work alone on calling for Gavin. Tristan tried first, with no results.

"How do I call him?" Sabrina asked.

"Will him to appear."

She closed her eyes. Within moments, Gavin stood in front of them. The large Scot's eyes widened at seeing Tristan. He stood without moving, barely acknowledging Sabrina with a slight nod.

"You're free." His words were stilted. "How can that be?"

"I am not sure." Tristan moved to him, placing his hand on his shoulder. "Has Gwyneth returned?"

"No. We were preparing to go seek assistance from the Princesses when you summoned me. We assumed Meliot had you as well."

"Go, seek guidance, but don't go to Meliot's castle just yet. I don't want any harm to come to either my daughter or Gwyneth. We must plan this well."

"Agreed," Gavin replied, and immediately disappeared.

"I was going to offer my assistance," Sabrina told him, throwing her hands up. "I'm going to bed; do you need anything?"

Tristan shook his head. Edith had already showed him where the large master bedroom was.

Alone again, he paced the room. If given a choice between his daughter and Gwyneth, he would have to pick his daughter.

What would happen to Gwyneth?

An act of kindness, saving those villagers so long ago, had come at a steep price. He was determined not to have to pay any more. There had to be a way to win.

Chapter Twenty-Nine

Iola used to tell them wonderfully intriguing stories, when they were little girls. The three sisters would eagerly go through their bedtime routines on those nights that Momma promised story time. Each story would pull them in, the characters brought to life by Momma's vivid descriptions and scenarios. Worlds were built and destroyed in their bedroom, the only sound besides their mother's voice gasps of surprise.

Now Gwen understood. Not only was story time a time of a loving mother spending time with her children, but also training. Once they became older, the stories continued, stories they knew by heart, but now their mother added more information. They learned that evil existed, just as there were good people in the world. They became intimately aware of the spirit world, spinning simple spells to help lost souls or keep evil ones away from the innocent.

To help, her mother told them, was their purpose. The

reason for the Lockhart women's existence—as it had been for ages.

When Gwen, the oldest, got the nerve to ask about their vast differences in appearance and coloring, their mother told them her story. She'd fallen in love with a mysterious man who'd come to her one day. She'd been seduced by his looks and ability to spin words into compliments like she'd never heard before. For years they'd been lovers, creating three vastly different-looking offspring. He'd insisted it was the way of his family as he'd come from a mixture of races. Then one day, he'd announced to her that his time with her was over. According to her mother, he'd seemed heartbroken, not willing to tell her where he went. And just like it had begun, one day he was gone.

Gwen racked her brain. Somewhere in one of her mother's lessons lay the answer to her current predicament.

Sitting on a tree trunk, she devoured the last of three apples, her first meal in two days. She'd been on the run since she'd panicked and vanished when Meliot ordered his wolves to seize her. Invisibility didn't stop her from being tracked, so she'd conjured up a flying spell and was able to float short distances, not very far above the ground, but high enough to keep her scent off the path, making her hard to track.

Weak after two days and nights of travel with no sleep, she was ready to give up. Nerves raw from avoiding capture, she'd tried different methods of reaching Meliot's castle undetected. Now, as she sat keeping an eye on said castle, the front door opened, and sentinels exited. They sniffed the air and trekked away from her. The wind was in her favor, or perhaps it was the constantly falling snow, covering scents and tracks. Finally, an opportunity.

She floated to the castle entrance and slipped inside. She'd find Clara, make the girl invisible, and hopefully take her to safety.

That was it. Her only plan.

Once inside, darkness loomed, making visibility hard. She strained to listen for voices, the sounds of the wind outside making it impossible. She went down long corridors, listening at doorways for the sound of a little girl. Most doors were silent. Hoping to feel the presence of the child, she opened her senses, moving along the hallway, once listening at a door, and a second time allowing her intuition to guide her.

A soft whimper caught her attention. She barely heard it over the sound of her rapidly beating heart. Freezing, she listened intently. The whimper sounded again, and she floated outside a door, trying to decide how to proceed. Feeling as if she had no choice, she reached for the doorknob. Footsteps sounded. Gwen opened the door and rushed inside, forgetting her invisibility. She stood inside the door, her head leaning on the wooden panel, waiting for the footsteps to pass by.

No sooner did the footsteps pass then the sound of another whimper caught her attention. A small child lay in a bed crying, her slight body shaking. Gwen became visible and approached the bed slowly. Although not tied up or bruised, the child's clothing was in tatters, her feet bare.

"Hey," Gwen whispered, trying not to startle the child. Shiny green eyes met hers. The eyes told it all. This was Clara.

"Hello, Clara," Gwen said, smoothing the girl's messy hair. "I'm here to take you to your daddy."

"Da? He's here?" Clara's bottom lip trembled. "He's finally come?"

"No, he's not here, but I know how to get you to him. You have to be very quiet. Promise me you won't make a sound," Gwen told the wide-eyed girl. She wanted to cry at the thought of this child being held for so long, forced to remain a little girl for hundreds of years. Meliot's heart was indeed black and evil.

Gwen wrapped the child in the blanket from the bed. It was not enough to keep her warm outside, but hopefully she'd be able to find Sterling quickly. "Hold on to my neck," Gwen instructed Clara. "Don't let go. We're going to be invisible—isn't that fun?" Clara nodded, a small smile curving her lips. She looked so much like Tristan it made Gwen's heart ache. "Here we go, shhh."

She floated out of the room, closing the door softly behind them. When they reached a second corridor, it was a dead end. Panicked, Gwen doubled back and turned the opposite way. This, too, became a dead end.

"You're here," Meliot's voice sounded behind her. "There is no escaping. Each time you turn down a corridor, it will become shorter and shorter until it will be easy to reach out and grab you."

She ignored the wizard, avoided looking at him, and flew down the corridor back towards the room. The hallway ended, much shorter than before. He hadn't lied.

They were trapped.

. . .

Panic always affected her in strange ways; her first reaction usually was to do something senseless. True to form, instead of giving up, Gwen ran straight into the wall in front of her. Clara screamed as they flew through the wall and straight out into the snow.

An illusion. Meliot's specialty.

They were outside. No time to celebrate, however, because she couldn't breathe. Landing on her stomach with the child on top of her, knocked the wind out of her. Not able to move, she waited for the suffocating feeling to go away. When she was finally able to take a gulp of air, she realized they were both visible again. The black sentinels saw them too, and ran towards them, growls filling the air.

Gwen jumped to her feet, grabbed the still-wrapped Clara and pushed the girl behind her, turning to face the wolves. The sentinels surrounded her, their luminous eyes locked on her, a terrifying barrier, even when keeping their distance. She had no doubt they were holding her for Meliot. She wasn't about to stand around and wait for the madman to appear.

Hopefully she'd be able to vanish again and float away with Clara. Gwen tried, nothing happened. When she tried the second time, they flickered, but didn't disappear.

"You can't disappear. Not now." Meliot stood before her. "My magic is much stronger than your feeble attempts." The wizard seemed to float above the snow as he neared them. "What have you got there?"

"We made a deal, you have to let her go," Gwen told him. "I'll stay, but Clara must be returned to her father."

The wizard stopped, frowning. "What are you talking about?"

"Clara," Gwen moved aside. The Wizard's eyes widened slightly, but he didn't speak. "I didn't trust you to release her, so I came to get her. I was taking her back to the knights' keep."

Meliot stepped closer, his soulless eyes pinned to the child, his lips curving into a twisted version of a smile. "A deal is a deal after all, isn't it?" He glanced at the sky. "The Icing comes. You and the child cannot make it far now. Not without freezing to death." He waved toward his castle. "Return inside and I'll ensure she is escorted back."

"The truth." What did Prince Sterling say about the truth? Gwen racked her brains.

Gwen noticed that he didn't get any closer. The amulet around her neck grew warm and she glanced down, it glowed. She narrowed her eyes at Meliot. "You can't touch me, can you? Not while I'm wearing this amulet."

Meliot glared, his black eyes narrowing. The malevolence in his expression gave her chills. The intensity of his stare traveled through her body. Her arms began to tingle. When her hands moved up to the leather strap around her neck, she fought against it, but couldn't stop her fingers from pulling the strap up over her head. With a shaky hand, she held the amulet out in front of her. Meliot did not make a move to take it from her. "Well, should I make you throw it? Or should perhaps you should just give it away?" Meliot motioned to one of the wolves.

Her legs gave out and she fell to her knees, hand still

outstretched. One of the wolves came and snatched the amulet out of her hand. He trotted away into the woods.

Meliot walked closer. "Now make her disappear. Enough with the parlor tricks."

"She's not a parlor trick. She's real."

"I know all about making beings appear, I have armies of them. Make her disappear and come with me now."

He turned and began walking back towards the castle. Gwen fought against her body, but she followed behind him willingly. "Clara come, stay right beside me," she whispered to the frightened little girl.

"Enough!" Meliot turned, his face transformed in rage. "Make her disappear now," he told her through clenched teeth.

"I can't."

"You can and you will. Or I will." He held his hand out to the now screaming Clara.

"No!" Gwen cried. "Look, please, just allow her to go home." Gwen began crying in desperation. "She's just a little girl."

Meliot froze. He peered at Clara again. "Where did you find her?"

"Inside your castle, in a room."

He scanned the wood line behind her. Gwen pulled Clara closer and tried to hush her. While Meliot was distracted, she tried to vanish again, but whatever ward he used kept her from being able to do so.

"What kind of trickery is this?" Meliot moved so fast Gwen didn't see him snatch Clara until he held the wincing girl up by her arm, her skinny legs dangling. "Answer me!" the wizard yelled into the air.

A bright light flashed at the point where Meliot held Clara. He released her.

Clara fell to the ground. Meliot stared at his singed hand.

Clara had powers!

Gwen hoped she could get away. If she could only get to her, but her feet refused to budge, and she almost fell forward trying to reach the child.

The child was quiet, lying on the ground without moving. Then Clara stood up, she began to grow and transform. She morphed into a lithe woman, dressed in long emerald-green robes, her features no longer favoring Tristan. Frosty blue eyes met Meliot's.

"Esmeralda, I should have known." Meliot took a step toward the woman, but she held up her hand, energy burst from her palm, and he flew backward. Meliot flashed back and returned with a blast of his own. It rippled around the woman, her hair and robes flying in the wind. "I'm warded, cousin."

She looked at Gwen. "You can move freely now."

Gwen tried and she indeed could. She went and stood next to Esmeralda.

"A deal is indeed a deal. I believe Tristan McRainey's enchantment has been broken. Gwyneth willingly sacrificed herself, was willing to trade places with his daughter out of love for him." Esmeralda told the wizard in a scolding tone. "My brother alerted me to this woman requiring help, and I decided to see about it myself."

She held out a hand, palm toward Meliot. "It ends now."

Astonishingly, Meliot bowed his head. "I will still win the war, dear cousin."

Esmeralda's expression was sorrowful. "I hope not."

She turned to Gwen. "Take my hand, I will return you to your world."

"Wait," Gwen told her. "Where's Clara?"

The woman looked over to Meliot, enraged. Then she turned with a distressed expression toward Gwen. "The child died in the forest that day."

Gwen took Esmeralda's hand, and they were gone.

Chapter Thirty

After Sabrina insisted he was not needed and required time alone, Tristan allowed his descendant, Edith, to dress him in something more suitable for the modern world.

Discomfort seemed to be the overall theme of the day. Tristan fought the urge to squirm in his seat as Calum McRainey leaned forward, studying him without regard for propriety, the old man's bulbous nose almost touching his. Tristan glowered down at the man.

"'Tis a shame that you were trapped for so long, Sonny." Calum tsked before turning to the other council members. As if speaking in court, he paced in front of the seated council members. One hand outstretched, with the other he pulled a timepiece out of his vest pocket and studied it before continuing.

"The young man is most definitely a McRainey. Has the McRainey build and carries himself in a manner that reminds me of my uncle Robert McRainey, God rest his soul. The resemblance cannot be denied." He referred to the late last Laird McRainey.

For hours now, each of the four elderly council members had taken turns, standing and speaking of what to do to prove who he was. Unfortunately, any information he'd given them was beyond their abilities to prove. After all, most of what he'd lived through happened almost four hundred years earlier. When he'd given them more modern facts he'd gathered from appearing in the estate, he was told the information could be easily gotten from an item called "internet."

"Perhaps you know something about this house that no one else would, dear." Edith's eyes were filled with compassion, when they met his. "Do you know of any estate secrets or maybe some inscriptions that could be unearthed?"

Tristan practically jumped to his feet. "Follow me." He left the room not looking back to see if they did. At this point, he wanted them gone so that he could get back to figuring out a way to save Clara and Gwyneth.

The council members appeared to be enjoying the possibility of being the ones to announce the "enchanted knight's" return, and didn't seem inclined to leave until they had the proof. The news would no doubt help them make their mark in Dunimarle Castle's history. He hurried through the kitchen and down a dimly lit hallway. At the end of the hallway was a small wooden door; the padlock barely protested when he yanked it open. His strength had not diminished upon returning, it seemed. He ignored the protests behind him as he jogged down some wooden stairs into a large wine cellar. Once in the cellar, he searched for something to provide light.

The room suddenly brightened. "Electricity," Derrick told him standing at the top step.

Tristan ignored him and went to the far wall. Once there he pushed the shelving full of wine bottles aside. The secret passage was there, but he couldn't remember which brick would open it. Steps sounded as the council members finally arrived, telling each other to take care as they descended. Clawing at several bricks, he finally took a step back and studied each one. He turned to Derrick. "Do you have something with a flame? A candle?"

Derrick nodded, went to a small table, and picked up a candlestick. "One would hate to be trapped down here without light." Using a match, he lit the candle and handed it to Tristan, who moved it across the wall until the flame flickered. He'd found it. He allowed Derrick to take the candle back then pulled at the brick. A door opened.

A collective gasp made him roll his eyes. "There are caves under here that take one to the seashore. It was used before my time for escaping if the keep was ever under siege. Only my Da and I knew about it. My Da told me there was no longer a need for it after the attacks from the Norse had ceased to be a threat. We had friendly relationships with neighboring clans... there was no longer a need for it."

"I'll go look," Derrick said, stepping through the narrow doorway. The young McRainey gave Tristan a skeptical glance. "After you, Cousin."

Tristan hoped the crates with his gold were still well hidden, as he stepped down the stone stairway. Although Derrick seemed to be accepting of his presence, trust would have to come with time. Tristan stopped at the bottom of the stairs glancing around the caves. He knew that two turns right would take them to the shoreline, three left, to his treasure.

Derrick sniffed the air. "I don't see any need to go any further. I can smell the salt air." The young man seemed to sense Tristan's apprehension because he paused and looked around. "I'm surprised no supplies were kept down here. Boats, oars, perhaps some food stuffs, and blankets."

"They were, but everything was removed before it was sealed." Tristan didn't move toward the stairs, not wanting to seem too eager.

Tristan looked around. "My Da told me he played down here as a child, but after one of his cousins drowned, his own da placed the wine shelves in front of the secret passageway. My Da showed me the passageway, since I was to become the laird. I tried to show my brother before... leaving, but we didn't have time."

The young McRainey began up the stairs. "Tragic."

The council finally left, satisfied that Tristan was who he claimed to be. Their anticipation of spreading the news was obvious. They began talking loudly as soon as they were outside, climbing into what Edith called an auto.

Glad for the interrogation to be over, Tristan sat. Leaning forward, he rested his face in his hands. He brushed his hair away from his face, exhaustion beginning to take over. He wore modern slacks and a buttoned-up blue shirt. The cloth they were made of, felt soft against his skin. The shoes he wore were comfortable, soft black leather. Derrick purchased many shirts, pants, under garments, and shoes, at

Edith's request. Deliverymen laden with packages arrived early that morning.

He felt overwhelmed. If not for the situation at hand, he'd want to find a horse and ride for hours. A hard ride was the best way to clear a man's head, the only way to truly find time alone.

"Tristan, you look tired, do you want to rest?" Edith placed a hand on his shoulder. "We should have waited to call the council, but I was afraid word would get out once the servants began talking."

"I'm glad it is over," Tristan replied. "I cannot rest, not until we hear back from the alter-world."

"What about the legal aspects of this?" Derrick asked his aunt. "I don't see how any judge will turn everything over to a man that supposedly was trapped in another world for centuries."

"You're correct," Edith faced her nephew, her face taut. "It might just come down to honor. You do know what that is, don't you?"

Affronted, Derrick did not reply to her question. "I have matters to attend to in town. I'll take my leave." He nodded at them and left.

"I don't want to distress you, Tristan, but he's not going to give up easily." Edith told him. "Ever since he's come up with this idea of transforming the estate into a resort, he won't listen to reason. But I've taken steps, to ensure you come into what is yours. Don't worry." The woman shook her head, a cocky smile on her face. "Derrick needs a wife and children. We need to settle him down. The boy has too much free time. Perhaps children would keep him out of trouble."

"Perhaps," Tristan replied, not totally convinced.

"Hallo, Tristan," Gavin's deep voice sounded behind them. "I've returned with Lady Gwyneth."

Tristan turned to see Gavin, who seemed to be in pain, as the large man was doubled over, barely holding himself upright. As Gavin stumbled forward, finally landing face-first onto the carpet, Tristan noticed Gwen. She held her hand to her mouth and ran from the room.

"Told her to keep those eyes closed," Gavin mumbled, not looking much better. Edith hurried after Gwen as Tristan helped Gavin to a large chair. "How did you get her back?"

"Esmeralda's men were bringing her to our keep as we headed to Meliot's castle. We met them on the road. They returned with us to the keep, and I immediately brought her back. We can actually leave the keep now, Meliot's minions are strangely absent."

"Where's Clara?"

Gavin shrugged and shook his head. "The lady said she would tell only you." The Scot leaned back closing his eyes. "I need a few moments. Movement between our worlds, as Padraig puts it, hurts like hell."

Running out of the room and up the stairs, Tristan burst into Gwyneth's bedroom. It was empty. Hearing voices, he turned and stormed into Sabrina's, where he found Gwen on the floor, sobbing in her sister's arms.

Face flushed, she cried, shaking as she clutched to her sister. "Oh God, I can't do it. I can't tell him the truth—he's been through enough."

Sabrina soothed her, her hand patting Gwen's back, while Edith poured a glass of water and placed it next to the sisters.

Edith glanced up at him and went to the window, bowing her head, eyes closed, she seemed to be praying.

Feeling as if he'd been drenched in ice water, Tristan couldn't wait. "Tell me," he told her, not moving closer to the women on the floor.

Gwen froze. She turned to him, her face flushed, her cheeks wet.

"Did you leave my daughter behind to save yourself?"

She opened her mouth, and her eyes rolled back. She fainted.

"You'll have to wait for your answer. Please leave," Sabrina snapped, as she and Edith went to the unconscious Gwen.

"Call the maid to come," Edith told him, her eyes pleading for him to be patient.

Chapter Thirty-One

Clara was still in Meliot's clutches. His daughter remained behind. Blinded by rage, Tristan made his way back to the study, needed to find Gavin. A maid came out of the study, took one look at him, and scurried past him without a word.

Gavin still sat on the chair; he looked up expectantly when Tristan entered. "Take me back now," Tristan told him, not caring that the Scot still seemed weakened. "I must go find my daughter. To hell with it all. I didn't want to come here and will gladly return." He grabbed at the Scot's shirt.

Frustration and fury mixed in Gavin's eyes as he removed Tristan's fisted hands from his shirt. "I can't take you. Esmeralda told us that once we come to this realm permanently, we can only return when a situation calls for it."

"This situation certainly does." Tristan shook, containing himself from punching anything nearby. "I'll make a deal with the devil himself to return. Summon Meliot and tell him I'll be his slave for eternity in exchange for Clara's freedom."

Standing before the fireplace, he placed a hand on the mantel. "Why, Gavin? Why have we paid such a high price for saving that village? Surely God would have compassion on us by now." He ignored the tears of frustration that streamed down his face.

"We shouldn't question our fate," Gavin replied, resigned. "I will return. We'll save her. You have my word on it. Meliot will die. He will pay a thousandfold for what he's done. Perhaps we won't be his punishers, but I pray we can witness his demise."

Tristan faced his friend. "Thank you."

"I must go, the pull is too strong for me to remain." Gavin stood, swaying slightly. "This is going to hurt."

Tristan nodded, understanding Gavin's reluctance to go through the leap. "I will talk to Gwyneth as soon as she awakens. I will ask her sister to send word. She seems to have a connection with you."

A look of almost panic crossed Gavin's face, but he quickly masked it. "I will return when there is news." He vanished.

"CAN YOU HEAR ME?" The words penetrated, sounding far away and then sharper, closer. "Gwen, look at me." Sabrina's face loomed over hers.

At once she remembered everything and sat up. The

room tilted, and she waited for the feeling to pass. "Where is Tristan?"

"I assume he's in his room. He's enraged, I would give him time to calm down."

"No, it's not fair to keep him waiting. I'll go to him now."

"I'll go with you."

"No." She slid off the bed and stood. Feeling steady, she ran her fingers through her hair. It was a tangled mess. She'd been in the same clothes since leaving, felt dirty. A shower would have to come first, then she'd find Tristan.

UPON ENTERING the dim master bedroom, she saw Tristan right away. As before, he stood by the window, hands clenching and unclenching. She turned to close the door behind her, gasping when Tristan took her arm.

"Talk." Fury seared from him. "Did you see Clara? How could you leave her?"

"Tristan, you're hurting me." She tried to push away from the door, but he was an immovable stone wall.

He would not accept anything but the truth. She remembered Sterling's words: *The best defense is truth.*

"Meliot never held Clara. Clara is dead... died in the woods. Meliot used the dreams to punish you. I thought I found Clara. I took a small girl from Meliot's castle and tried to escape. I made it outside. He caught us. When he saw her, he seemed surprised, shocked. He accused me of creating her. An illusion. I begged him to release her and take me in her place. Then the little girl transformed into Esmeralda. She forced his hand, told him the rules of the enchantment were broken. That he had to release me. I asked what happened to Clara. Esmeralda told me Meliot had tried to take her that day, the day in our dreams. She fell into a ravine whilst running from him and died."

His body tensed. He didn't move away. Instead he stood still as a statue.

"No!" A guttural roar emanated from him.

Turning from her, he walked in a circle; head lowered, he pushed the heels of his hands into his eyes.

"For so many years, I dreamed of her and wondered. I held on to the hope she was alive." His voice was hoarse, strangled.

Gwen wanted to go to him, comfort him, but was unsure he wanted anything other than to allow his grief to consume him.

What if it did? What if not giving him some sort of solace had an adverse effect?

She closed her eyes and took a deep breath sensing all his pain. When she opened them, he stood next to the bed, his shoulders shaking.

Unable to stop herself, she rushed to him, wrapped her arms around him and began pressing kisses to his wet face. "Allow me to take some of your pain, Tristan."

He began blindly tearing her clothes off. The garments fell in shreds at her feet in quick succession until she was fully nude before him. She lifted her face to him and his mouth took hers. Soon his clothes joined hers on the floor.

Muscles rippled, as he seemed to struggle with himself.

Gwen ran her hand down the side of his face. "I am here for you."

Darkened green eyes met hers as he easily lifted her. Wrapping her legs around him and crossing ankles, she let out a moan when he entered her.

Passion collided with sorrow; she felt his pain and sadness flow through them with each thrust of his hips, Tristan's silence so different from the other times they'd made love. But this wasn't making love, this was a reaction to shock, a release of emotions too large to contain.

When his pace increased, he moved in and out of her, his movements smooth but frantic. Gwen allowed herself to let go. Tristan growled, the sound not too different than that of a wounded beast as he gushed into her, his large body shaking in release.

He went to the bed and lowered them both onto it where they remained locked together for a long while, his head resting beside hers, their breathing the only sound in the room. Finally, he slid out of her and stood.

"I apologize. Please, I need to be alone."

"No apology needed," Gwen replied, forcing herself not to offer him comfort. The pain in her chest took her breath away. Her heart was breaking. Not only was she losing the only man she'd ever loved, but she was leaving a broken man behind. He couldn't love her now. She'd be a constant reminder of so much grief.

Her clothes beyond repair, she went to the bathroom and grabbed a towel. Wrapping it around her, she walked out.

Tomorrow they would talk.

Then she'd return to Georgia.
Her job here was done.

Chapter Thirty-Two

The next day was a brisk, sunny day. Gwen strolled through the garden in the back of the McRainey estate. She pulled her wrap closer and glanced up to Edith walking toward her. The woman held out her hand. Gwen took it.

"Come, let us sit," Edith told her, pulling her to a wooden bench. "I can't remember such a beautiful morning this early in the spring." She studied Gwen for a beat. "I know you are planning to leave. You shouldn't make a hasty decision."

"I think it would be better for him if I do leave," Gwen replied, looking toward the house. "He needs time to get accustomed to everything."

"Tristan does need time, time to mourn, time to adjust and learn new things," Edith agreed. "However, I also think he has strong feelings for you, and if you leave, it will be one more thing he'll have to cope with. I ask you to reconsider. I know it's not easy for you either."

Before standing, the older woman patted her hand. "Now, I'd better go ensure a meal is taken up to him. Think on what I've said."

Would remaining help? One thing for sure, she was too confused to think straight. She'd never been in love before, didn't know until the day before that heartbreak actually did hurt physically. After leaving Tristan's room, she'd fallen into her bed and cried herself to sleep. Not just because she was losing him, but she ached thinking of how much he was hurting. Love was an incredible thing. She'd never make light of a person in love again.

She'd awakened to find Sabrina walking in with a cup of hot tea. Her insightful sister also brought toast and a new box of tissues. Gwen immediately began crying again, telling Sabrina everything, each detail of the past several weeks. Repeating everything out loud tore her inside out.

Sabrina listened without comment, handing her tissues and pushing the tea into her hands when hiccups began. After nibbling on the toast, she collapsed back onto the pillows exhausted, but glad to have gotten everything out.

Like Edith, Sabrina insisted she remain in Scotland, at least for another couple of weeks. Her sister was flying to England for a two-week photo shoot, and promised to return afterwards so they could fly back home together.

Two weeks. Too long to be in the same house with the man you loved, who didn't want to see you. And yet not long enough in the knowledge you'd never see him again.

"Good morning, Gwen." Derrick walked down the garden path toward her. "Aunt Edith told me I could find you here."

For a moment Gwen's heart skipped. Derrick had the same build as Tristan, although Derrick's hair had auburn highlights, and his eyes were dark brown, the two men could be brothers. Unlike other times she'd seen him, Derrick, who prided himself in an impeccable appearance, had his hair mussed, his shirt untucked. He sat next to her, and looked off into the distance, a serious expression on his handsome face.

"This place is full of bad memories for my uncle. I think the best course for him is to begin a new life. He has much to learn, too much to deal with without the added constant reminders of this place. Would you consider convincing him to move to America with you?"

She started to speak. He held up his hand silencing her. "If both of us of convince Aunt Edith this is for his own good, then the three of us can talk him into it. Especially right now. He is not doing well. I just came from seeing him and had to leave the room. The madman attacked me."

Not stopping to think, Gwen slapped Derrick hard across the face. "How could you?" She yelled at him. "After all that he's gone through you still want to take his home away from him!" Angry, she jumped to her feet. "Derrick, you are inconsiderate and materialistic, still trying to come up with ways to get this estate."

Derrick remained frozen, his hand on his reddened jaw, eyes bulging at her. "I don't have to take this," he spat at her. "Legally, I take control of the estate next year, there is no way for him to prove to be who he is. He may have convinced those old fools on the city council, but no judge in Scotland will grant him ownership."

He stood glaring at her. "I don't know why I bothered.

Tell Aunt Edith, she'll be hearing from my lawyers sooner than expected. When I tell them she wants to leave the estate to a dead man, they'll grant me ownership right away." He spun on his heel and stormed around to the front of the house, to where his Ferrari, Jaguar, or Lamborghini was no doubt parked.

Gwen caught movement in a window on the second floor; the curtain fell back into place. It was Tristan's room.

He'd watched the exchange between her and Derrick. She wondered what he made of it.

She considered going and trying to talk to him, but decided to go find Sabrina instead. She'd stay, especially now. Edith and Tristan would be needing her if the case was indeed brought up before the legal system.

Blowing out a frustrated breath, she headed inside.

Chapter Thirty-Three

"There are many duties to attend to; you cannot remain in this self-imposed confinement any longer." Edith McRainey was a force to be reckoned with, confirmation that he'd made the right decision when leaving his estate in the hands of McRainey women through the decades.

He sat on the bed, without any motivation to do anything.

Standing before him now, the slight woman did not allow for excuses of any kind. "This is three days now you have remained holed up in this room. The estate will not run itself, you know. Decisions must be made regarding the renovations to the stables, reinforcing the fencing in the west pasture, and someone needs to check on the progress of the farmers who've been reluctant to follow my orders."

The last statement he had a hard time believing; nonetheless, he allowed her to continue. "I understand you've been through a great deal, and face plenty of challenges ahead. However, time does not stand still. You don't have the luxury of wallowing."

Tristan frowned, "I'm sure everything is well in hand without any help from me. Somehow the estate managed, and verra well without me."

"So everything was for naught?" Edith took his jaw and pulled his face up to look at her. "Clara died—bless the poor child's soul. You deserve to mourn, believe me I understand. I have experienced the pain of losing a child. I lost a son."

Tristan was shocked, not remembering ever seeing a boy about since Edith took residence. "Don't be so shocked. I was in love once, and would have married my son's father, if not for being so foolish when young.

"Now," she said, placing her hands on her slim hips. "You have an estate to run, responsibilities to assume, and more importantly, your friends' hopes of freedom are pinned on your shoulders. The staff is waiting downstairs to meet you. Come down at once."

If not for the constant noise provided by what they called a *telly* in the corner of the room, Tristan knew he'd hear his heart thumping, the fast beats not unlike those of anger. Edith was right; he had duties to attend to.

He'd mourn in private, on his own time. Once standing, his gaze was drawn back to the moving pictures in the telly, a woman was speaking of world news. It was that new world that had his heart pounding harder, faster. Honestly, the thought of leaving the room terrified him.

Descending the stairs, Tristan was surprised to see there were only six staff members lined up. Two, both maids, he'd met before, as they'd brought him meals, the other four were men.

Beaming, Edith stepped up to him, putting her hand on this arm. "I'd like to formally introduce you to my son, Tristan McRainey, who will assume total control of the family estates and holdings, as of today." Curious looks were directed at him, but none of the staff members seemed shocked that Edith had a son. Unlike them, Tristan was sure his expression gave away his surprise at her introduction.

Edith continued unabated, introducing him to both maids, Hannah and Liza, followed by three men, Ross, Cameron, and Duncan, whose duties included grounds keeping and stables, and Miles Sullivan, foreman of the estate. Sullivan, a large man, was the only one to step forward and shake his hand. "Laird, it's a pleasure to finally meet you." The older man nodded toward the other men. We look forward to working with you."

"Please call me Tristan," he replied. Ensuring to keep his face neutral, he shook each person's hand, asking about their family and length of employment.

After the staff left the hallway, only Miles remained. The older man chuckled and shook his head. "I take it Ms. Edith didn't tell you she planned to introduce you as her son." He gave Edith a warm smile.

Edith sniffed in response, "I didn't have a chance, I was too busy beating sense into the boy."

"Why did you introduce me as your son?"

"In this, Derrick is correct. People have an easier time believing that I had a son out of wedlock who lived abroad with his father his entire life, than they would in believing you came back from a four-hundred-year enchantment."

Miles nodded, drinking from his coffee cup. "Miss Edith here has been mentioning a son for years now, in preparation of your return."

"Thank you," Tristan told his new mother, who waved it away.

"Let's do a tour of the estate, shall we?" she told them. "I'm anxious to retire to my flat in town. Finally, I can join my girlfriends for tea and shopping without having to worry about things at the estate taking all my time and attention."

Gwen entered the room, her journal and pen in hand. She didn't meet his eyes but smiled warmly at both Miles and Edith.

"I'm glad you're joining us. We're about to begin the tour of the estate lands and will definitely enjoy having your company," Edith told Gwen, linking arms with her and leading her towards the front door. "We've so much to do and see—your notes will come in handy for Tristan."

"Beautiful lady," Miles told Tristan, walking beside him as they followed the women out. "If only I were about thirty years younger." He chuckled at Tristan's glare. "Of course, you don't have that obstacle, do you?"

Tristan almost smiled. He liked the man.

Tristan assisted Gwen into a large golf cart. When his hand held her elbow, she visibly flinched at his touch. The distance between them didn't settle well with him.

"Are you well?" he asked her, only to receive a curt nod in response. He climbed into the large golf cart, in front next to Miles, while the women settled into the back seat.

He was astounded at the many changes to the estate, but the lay of the land remained the same. He began to recognize landmarks Miles pointed out and found himself relaxing, releasing his death grip on the handlebar in front of him.

He now owned less land; just over a thousand acres surrounded the home and cottages. When they stopped atop a ridge that overlooked the estate and stables, Gwen seemed to soften, joining in asking questions, jotting down notes and even laughing as they watched two foals at play.

At the stables, he meandered, stopping at each stall, studying each horse. The beasts were of good stock. He was pleased with Miles' choices. Edith went into a small room that Miles called an office, and he was left alone. Stroking a large black horse, he decided to ride him later.

Going outside behind the stables, he was greeted by noisy pens housing pigs and goats. Gwen didn't notice him approaching as she patted a goat's head, speaking to the animal softly.

"Aren't you cute," Gwen cooed at the animal, which preened, nuzzling her hand.

"You like beasties?"

She nodded. "I do prefer the smaller ones. Although I do like horses, I prefer smaller animals, like dogs, cats, and, well, now goats." She smiled at the goat, allowing him to nuzzle her arm.

"We must speak," he told her. "I would like to begin work to free the remaining men immediately."

"Of course," she replied, finally raising her eyes to him. He felt his heart tighten at the tenderness in them.

"I have an idea about Gavin. I think he and my sister connected."

"I do as well," Tristan agreed, moving closer, but stopping when she took a step back. Not wanting to make her uncomfortable, he turned toward the stables. "After the evening meal, we can adjourn to the sitting room."

THE DAY PROGRESSED QUICKLY. After touring the estate lands, Tristan locked himself up in the study with Edith and Miles to begin lessons on running the estate. They'd decided to spend two hours a day teaching him.

Edith was pleased. "You're a quick study. I am impressed. You must have kept a close eye on how things were run while away."

"I would like to go for a ride this afternoon," Tristan told them, hiding how overwhelmed he felt at the moment.

"Son, you don't ask for permission, you do as you wish," Edith told him with fervor. "You are the laird. The sooner you are able to take the reins, the sooner my life of leisure begins." She giggled, a schoolgirl-like sound. "I can't wait."

GWEN PACED in the study after dinner. Tristan was not present at the beginning of the evening meal; he'd returned late from riding and burst into the room at the end of the meal, his eyes bright.

He'd apologized to Edith for his delay. Brushing his long hair impatiently away from his flushed face, he'd refused to sit at the table, claiming to be too soiled from his ride. It had been impossible not to admire him. Tall, dark, and handsome, not to mention his body. Tight riding pants displayed his muscular legs. The riding jacket showcased his broad shoulders. Gwen had been forced to look away, the tightness in her chest reminding her, she'd leave soon.

"Thank you for waiting." His entrance made her stomach pitch nervously.

She forced a smile. "Did you eat?"

"Nay, Liza is bringing something here," he replied, locking gazes with her.

Clearing her throat, Gwen opened her laptop. "While Sabrina was here, she spent time researching spells. She has strong seer abilities, which will prove helpful."

They spent the next hours going over details, even continuing while he ate. She was astounded by how much Tristan knew about each man in the alter-world. No doubt, they'd spent much time sharing the most intimate of details of their lives. She took notes on a laptop, biting back a smile when Tristan peered over her shoulder, frowning at the screen.

"What will happen to the words inside the frame?" he asked her, his brow still crinkled.

"It's stored in here," she told him, pointing at the bottom of the laptop. "I can plug it into another device called a printer, which will print my notes out to look like this." She picked up a piece of printed paper.

He held the paper, but didn't look at it. Instead his worried eyes met hers. "Through the years when I came here,

I tried to learn as much as I could. Each time I visited, much changed. I didn't realize it, but once I didn't come for almost fifty years. I felt lost. Parts of the house had been redone, some of the rooms enlarged, everything was totally different."

He took a deep breath. "I knew it would be difficult but didn't expect to not know basic things."

Gwen reached to touch his shoulder, but pulled her hand back. "Don't be so hard on yourself. The world, no matter how much times goes by, basically stays the same. I bet during your day women competed to look prettier than others; men favored certain knights in bouts, and argued with one another over who was superior. Young people sneaked kisses, children gave the food they didn't like to the dogs, and old people claimed the wisdom of time. Am I right?"

Finally his lips curved, "Yes, you are right. Knights in bouts?" He chuckled. "I do know about football. I've watched by a window, during family gatherings, as they kicked the ball about the pitch."

Glad he felt better, she saved the document on the computer and went to leave. He held her back, his hand on her forearm.

"There is something else we should discuss."

"Oh?"

"I've given my word to your sister. I do not wish to dishonor you. We've been intimate on more than one occasion. I will marry you.

"Oh, God."

How does one go about explaining the whole 'honor'

thing to a knight, without sounding like a total slut? Torn between wanting to laugh hysterically, throw herself into his arms screaming 'yes!' or running from the room, Gwen frowned at him.

"Tristan, do you believe me? About Clara?"

"Aye, deep inside I always knew she died that day in the forest."

That put to rest, she had to ask. "Did my sister say I had to marry you?"

"Aye," he replied, his eyes questioning.

There it was. The only reason he asked was because he felt he had to. Damn Sabrina— why hadn't she warned her of their conversation?

He came up behind her. "I know I don't have much to offer you, but..."

This time a bark of laughter escaped, as she always tended to do when overwhelmed by events.

Nothing to offer? Just filthy rich, handsome beyond words, a laird, great in bed—well, amazing in bed—not to mention she was in love with him.

"Are you all right?" Tristan's confused words sent her into peals of laughter, so loud Edith entered the room.

Gwen turned to face the woman and tried to speak, waving her hands, not making any sense. Finally, seeing the somber faces forced her to stop laughing. Sniffing she took a breath, wiping her eyes. "I'm sorry, I laugh when overwhelmed. Edith, can you please explain the nature of modern relationships to your... er, son?"

She giggled again. "He thinks he has to marry me for honor."

Edith became stern. "Come sit down, both of you." She sat on a large couch where they joined her, on either side.

"Tristan, you do not have to marry Gwen, even if you've been intimate. I assume you have, and that is why you're asking, am I correct?"

She waited until Tristan, who frowned at Gwen, nodded. "People marry for love mostly, nowadays."

"'Tis not reason to laugh," he contended.

Edith gave Gwen a pointed look before turning back to Tristan. "That is true, but don't take offense. It's nerves, not mirth."

"Now, Gwen," Edith spoke to her, tapping her knee. "Are you of modern thought that you'll only marry someone that suits?"

Sober now, Gwen replied, deciding to be honest. "I will only marry someone I am in love with and who loves me."

"There now." Edith got up, leaving while she and Tristan watched her. "Now, tell him *no*, since I take it he didn't profess to love you."

"WHAT DO you mean you said *no*," Sabrina's voice went up several octaves and forced Gwen to hold the phone away from her ear. "But you love him!"

"The only reason he asked was because you told him he had to. As a matter of fact, he didn't ask. He *stated* that he would marry me. He is doing the honorable, knightly thing." Gwen huffed impatiently. "Why didn't you tell me of this conversation, Sabrina?"

Her sister's giggle infuriated her. "All right, I admit I did say he had to marry you, but I also said to ask only if he loved you."

"Really?"

"Yes, really."

Chapter Thirty-Four

"We are 51% owners of McRainey Industries. Our finances are managed by Barron's Asset Management. We have holdings in Scotland Bioresearch and Aer Lingus. We bank at The Bank of Scotland, with additional accounts at Allied. The McRainey Estate is self-sufficient, sustained by earnings from horse-breeding and our crops. My net worth is just over seventy million." Tristan recited, pacing the length of the large office. His aunt nodded, occasionally glancing down at notes.

"Tell me about yourself."

"Tristan Ronan McRainey, I am two and...," he corrected himself, "I am thirty-two years old. I lived abroad most of my life, traveling constantly with my father's family, anthropologists, and therefore have little hands-on knowledge of modern technology. Never been married, no children..." He stopped speaking when someone knocked at the door.

Hannah entered and handed him an envelope, picked up the empty tea service, and left. They'd received a summons.

Derrick was filing a motion to freeze McRainey Estate's assets, maintaining that Edith intended to commit fraud in order to keep him from taking over the estate and its holdings.

"My nephew is mistaken if he thinks this foolishness will succeed." Edith's sharp eyes snapped to his. "We're to meet them in Edinburgh tomorrow. Well, this is a good time for you to meet with our financial manager. Let's put the last three days to practice."

ON HIS WAY to the stables, Tristan spied Gwen. Dressed in tight pants and a sleeveless blouse, she jogged away from him. She didn't see him. He wondered what she ran from, didn't see anything or anyone chasing her. He sprinted after her, calling her name. She didn't turn, perhaps she was in a trance. Reaching her, he grabbed her arm.

"Eeek!" Gwen screamed, slapping at him frantically. Eyes wide, she screamed a second time setting his ears to ringing. "You just scared the shit out of me," she exclaimed, pulling white items that hung from strings from her ears.

"I called you—you were running…" he began.

"I am jogging, for exercise… it's like training." She huffed, picking up the white items and showing them to him. "I couldn't hear you because I'm listening to music. Here let me put this near your ear." She touched the white bud to his ear, and he heard the soft notes of music.

"Why are you training? Do you expect to be chased?"

Her smile was the first one directed at him in many days. "No, I want to remain slender. I do it to keep from gaining weight. It's not attractive to be plump nowadays. I like to eat, so I have to exercise."

He frowned then asked. "What if your husband told you he preferred you to be plump?"

"That man would be my hero." Gwen beamed at him. "But most men these days prefer skinny women."

Tristan wanted to argue the poin; although he found no fault with Gwen's body, he decided it was best to remain silent. "Are women attracted to slender men as well?"

Her eyes skimmed over him, before looking up at him. Something stirred in his chest. "Men are measured differently, er... your body is the ideal." She blushed and looked away.

"Men don't have to be thin, as long as they don't have a huge belly," she rounded her arms in front of her stomach. "You don't have to worry too much."

He racked his brain for some type of compliment to give her. He'd never been one to court. Not even his betrothed. It was arranged, and the two times he'd met the lass, she'd been too busy talking about herself the entire time to pay him much heed. He tried to remember the words to songs the minstrels would sing about love, but came up empty. Finally he had a thought.

"I think you're perfectly fit to be any man's wife." Her confused look confirmed his lack of courting skills.

"Oh. Well. Thank you?" Gwen stammered. "I better finish my run, and let you get back to whatever it is you were about to do."

"Wait," Tristan told her. She hesitated with a curious

expression. "What I meant to say is that I think you are beautiful."

Shock registered on her face, followed by a tender look that made him want to continue complimenting her.

"Really?"

He nodded, not sure what else to say. "Yes, verra much so."

"Thank you." Gwen's smile brightened. "I'll see you later." She turned and ran away.

As she went away from him, he shook his head. Women were strange creatures. Why would she be surprised that he found her attractive? Being in the same house and not sharing her bed was proving harder and harder each day. Even so, he'd not been tempted once to tup the maid. Although Miles had pointed out to him that it was no longer a practice for the laird to tup the maids. Maybe he should tell Derrick, as he'd seen Hannah leaving his room at night.

Hearing noise behind him, he looked up to see Miles driving up on the cart. The foreman nodded at him. "Wondered where you took off to. The Stuarts have arrived. They're here to look at the silver stallion and discuss breeding."

Tristan looked once again toward where Gwen had run off, before climbing onto the cart.

Perhaps he'd ask Miles how one went about modern courting. He wanted to court Gwen.

She would not be leaving Scotland if he had anything to do with it.

Miles' robust laughter filled the small space in the stables, "My goodness, it's been many years since I've tried to win the affections of a lass." The older man refilled his beer, shaking his head in mirth. "You'd be better off asking Lord Derrick. He's very successful with the ladies."

Tristan drank the bitter liquid, not sure if he liked it. "I doubt Derrick will want to discuss courting with me. We're to go to Edinburgh to meet with him and his solicitor tomorrow."

"I see. Well, let me think," Miles rubbed his chin. "Ah, Duncan, there you are boy, come here. I have questions to ask of you." The other staff member gave them a puzzled look before walking over.

For the next several hours, the men, including Ross and Cameron who'd pulled up crates to sit on, tried to teach him which things to say to a woman and which were not acceptable.

When the men dispersed, Tristan found his way to bed. Woozy from drinking more beer than he should have, Tristan wondered if he'd remember everything they'd try to teach him and in the right order.

He'd enjoyed the time with the men in the stables. With a pang of guilt, he wondered what his friends, still trapped in the enchantment, were dealing with.

Chapter Thirty-Five

Entering Barron's, Derrick dodged the receptionist, who narrowed her eyes at him when she spotted him entering the lobby. Women never forgot the man that didn't call when he'd said he would. It was already a bad enough day without adding drama. The elevator doors closed just as he reached them. He pounded the up button to stop them, but it was too late.

"Well hello, Derrick McRainey," the woman, Lillian was her name, caught up to him. "You're not trying to avoid me, are you?"

Assuming a look of surprise, he faced her. "Lillian, what a pleasant surprise." He took her hand and squeezed it to his chest. "I have thought of you often. I know you won't forgive me for not calling, but I do hope you'll allow me to take you out for lunch after my meeting to, in part, make up for my abominable behavior."

Indecision was evident as she looked at their intertwined fingers. "Of course, I understand if you say no." He gave her his best sorrowful look, and any chance of refusal was dashed.

The elevator doors opened, and he entered, his eyes locked with Lillian's until the doors closed. Better to keep Barron's staff in his corner, especially after the morning he'd have.

His solicitor called first thing and rescheduled their appointment with Edith, telling him she'd filed a motion against him, calling for Derrick to cease and desist any actions against her holdings, based on irrefutable evidence that Tristan McRainey was her son. Being that the McRainey fortune always passed to the women of the family, if she proved Tristan was her son, it trumped Derrick, who was born to a McRainey male.

"Her son." He couldn't help but grumble out loud.

Usually he preferred not to attend the meetings with their financial manager, but today he was making an exception. Regardless of his lack of attendance, he understood business. He had graduated from Harvard and kept abreast of all the McRainey corporation transactions and holdings. It would be somewhat of a lift to the dreadful day to see Tristan make a fool out of himself at this meeting.

Derrick walked into Barron's Investment's large conference room and was promptly greeted by O'Donnell, their account manager. Only the man practically threw his hand back upon Edith and Tristan's entrance. The thin man's face beamed as he fawned over Derrick's aunt and her 'son.' Derrick sat and motioned for the assistant to pour him coffee as he waited for the butt-kissing episode to end.

He had to admit the change in his 'cousin' amazed him.

In a black Armani suit, Tristan looked every bit the business magnate. His hair, shorter, but still longer than most men's, was styled and combed away from his face.

If either Edith or Tristan were surprised at Derrick's presence, they did not show it. His aunt sat down across from him, allowing Tristan to sit at the head of the table. Tristan spoke to him first. "Hello, Derrick. Will you be joining us for dinner tonight? We'll be staying here in town for the evening."

Although shocked at the invitation, he tried to keep his expression flat. "I've other plans, thank you." He eyed his aunt, who smiled at him warmly.

Passing out leather portfolios with documents, O'Donnell began briefing them, interjecting enough details to ensure Tristan was brought up to date. Derrick noted that Tristan took notes the entire time.

The assistant announced the arrival of Colin Byrne, the owner of a small company they maintained a partnership with. Byrne proceeded to brief them on his company's current production and financial status.

Derrick interrupted him. "Byrne Inc. has shown a loss for the last three quarters. I don't see why McRainey Industries should maintain the partnership and continue financially assisting your failing business."

Colin Byrne looked to Edith and Tristan before speaking. "I stand behind my company and have no doubt that we will rise above our current set-back. The recession has caused the demise of many small companies such as Byrne Inc., but we've managed to survive. We're a strong Scottish company."

"Perhaps due to your strong partnership," Derrick told the man, noting his color rising.

"Mr. O'Donnell," Tristan interrupted. "Can you tell me if McRainey Industries has suffered any losses due to the recession?"

O'Donnell nodded. "Yes, my lord. But of course, most of your holdings are in safe accounts."

"I understand you can't give me specifics since it's a family matter, but have our losses with Byrne Inc. been worse than with other partners, big or small?"

"No."

Tristan looked to Colin Byrne. "We will maintain our partnership with you."

DERRICK STORMED out of the elevator, coming to a stop only when spotting the receptionist desk. The devil with Barron's. Today he could not care less if any receptionist was angry with him. He rushed out the side door of the building and straight to his car.

If Tristan and Edith were here in Edinburgh, that left Gwyneth home alone.

His fake cousin was infatuated with the ghost whisperer. Losing Gwen to Derrick, even if just a perception, would be a blow.

Or maybe just enough to make him feel better.

It was a perfect evening, as far as Gwen was concerned. Reading a romance novel in the study, lying on a couch before a cheerful fire, she couldn't help but sigh happily while allowing her gaze to scan the room. *This could be my home.* If only.

The recurring inner struggle regarding Tristan's proposal began. Yes, he didn't love her, but maybe in time he would. He definitely desired her. She loved him, and that counted for something. Didn't it?

No, she'd done the right thing. She would not say yes, not to his marriage proposal. Although, she wasn't sure she could resist him when it came to any other type of proposition. Shivering, she recalled their intimate times together. How she missed his touch.

The maids were off for the evening, so hearing the front door close, she sat up to see who'd arrived. Edith called earlier to tell her she and Tristan were remaining in Edinburgh. She planned to continue his business lessons all day, visiting some of McRainey's businesses. They'd stay in one of their Edinburgh homes for the night.

"Good evening, Gwen." Derrick walked in, making a beeline for the couch she was sitting on, dropping next to her. He gave her a charismatic smile she suspected was the downfall of many women. "I wanted to assure you, I hold no grudge over the incident in the garden. I was out of line."

"I'm glad," she replied, placing the book between them. "Edith and Tristan are not home. They're in Edinburgh."

"Pity," he told her, although his bright smile contradicted his statement. "Although, it gives me the opportunity to spend time with you. And get to know you better."

What was the man up to? Gwen fidgeted, unsure what to do. Pulling her hair up, she repositioned her clip, allowing it to remain in a messy up-do.

Derrick seemed to sense her discomfort and stood to pour himself a drink. With his rather tall whiskey in hand, he began to tell her of his exploits while attending Harvard. Before long she began to relax, enjoying the man's company.

Before long, both of them were laughing, comparing college stories. Gwen drank several glasses of wine. Admittedly, he could be charming when he wanted to.

"Goodness, it's almost one-thirty in the morning," Gwen told him, shaking her head. "I'd better get to bed."

Derrick nodded in agreement. "I'm afraid I drank too much to drive home. I will sleep here as well. A shame really to sleep in that huge empty bed all by myself." He leaned forward as if to kiss her, she turned away, laughing at his attempt.

He gave her a hurt look. "Gwen, a beautiful woman like you should never sleep alone."

"I don't always sleep alone," she replied, arching a brow. "I do have to admit, I understand how you are rarely by yourself in bed."

He bowed, smiling good-naturedly at her.

"Good night, Derrick," she told him, making her way to her room.

"Yes, good night to you as well," the response came.

Groggy, Gwen blinked as a sunray hit her face. She blinked, wondering why her curtain was thrown open.

Rolling over to reach for her cell phone, she bumped into the man lying next to her.

"What the hell are you doing here?" Gwen shrieked at the still sleeping Derrick.

He sprang up, his hair standing comically all over his head. "What?"

"Get out of my bed, you beast!" She began beating the dazed man, who fell off the bed, yelping in pain.

"When did you sneak in here? I told you *no*!" She picked up her pillow and continued beating him, not allowing him to get up. Finally he stopped trying to sit up and covered his face with his arms.

"You will get out of this room, and you will never, and I repeat *never* speak to me again. Do you hear me?" Gwen was becoming winded, but didn't stop the pillow beating.

"What in the bloody hell is your problem?" Derrick yelled at her. "I have a right to any room in this house."

"The hell you do." Tristan's angry voice caused Gwen to freeze, the pillow above her head. Derrick also froze, his wide eyes looking up at the very angry man who proceeded to pick the younger McRainey up and toss him across the room like a rag doll.

"Oh, shit." Gwen said, not sure what else fit the bill at a time like this.

Tristan crossed the room so swiftly he was a blur. Gwen jumped from the bed, managing to grab on to his arm as he reared back, his fist balled. Derrick was pinned against the wall, eyes bulging.

"Stop, Tristan. You'll kill him." Her feet lifted from the

floor as he swung. But he managed to stop just as he was about to connect with Derrick's jaw.

Tristan snarled in anger, his entire stance reminding her of his warrior training. "Do not leave. I will speak with you," he gritted out, shoving Derrick toward the doorway. "If you leave, I will comb the world looking for you and when I find you..." He didn't continue, as the younger McRainey held up his hands understanding.

Gwen released his arm, not sure what to do next. "You kept your strength."

"It would seem so." He looked her over as if to ensure she wasn't hurt.

Hair mussed from sleeping, straps falling off her shoulders, she made for a bewitching sight. "Did he touch you?"

She frowned at him. "No. He must have snuck in here while I slept. I don't think it was an accident, but I also don't think he would have forced himself on me."

Dragging his gaze away from her, he looked over to the rumpled bed. "I'm not so sure about that. I don't think he would have succeeded. It seems you were defending yourself in a manner that would dissuade any man from forcing himself upon you."

He pressed his lips together to keep from laughing, recalling the scene he'd walked into. She frowned up at him.

"You think it's funny. Augh! Get out."

"Do you really wish me to?" He asked her, moving closer.

"Yes?" She went to turn away. He held her arm. "You don't sound sure."

When her dark-brown eyes met his, the room seemed to tilt. If he didn't leave her bedroom, he might suffer the same fate as Derrick. Before she could protest, he kissed her lightly and turned.

"Why did you return so early?" Gwen stopped him.

"Your sister arrives today, does she not?"

She nodded.

"I am anxious to begin the work of freeing the men. I must go speak to Derrick. I wish to speak with you before your sister arrives."

When he entered the study, Derrick visibly tensed. Good, he wanted the young McRainey to feel intimidated. He, on the other hand, felt like the father about to punish an unruly child. Keeping his eyes flat, he stood, his hands relaxed at his side.

"I don't owe you anything, Derrick. Everything you have, the privileges you enjoy, are all because of the hard work of me, my Da, and his father before him. You will leave this house and not return until you accept that I am the rightful owner—Laird McRainey, rightful owner of Dunimarle Castle."

"It's just that…" Derrick began, but stopped talking when Tristan glared at him.

"If I had not left, been enchanted, I would have sired children. This entire debacle would not be an issue. You would have no claim whatsoever to my title or my lands." He crossed the room standing directly in front of Derrick. "You will leave this home now. Let everything you touch and come across remind you where it came from. Return only when you accept me as the laird."

Derrick met his eyes, defiance still there. Tristan almost smiled. "You are brash and impulsive—remind me of my younger brother, Geale. He grew up to become a strong leader, so I suspect you will too."

With one last questioning look, Derrick didn't reply, walking around Tristan, he left.

Chapter Thirty-Six

After returning from her afternoon jog, Gwen went to her room to shower.

Rinsing shampoo from her hair, she closed her eyes. The image of Tristan came to mind. The morning prior, she'd been struck speechless, barely able to eat, when he'd walked into the dining room for breakfast before leaving for Edinburgh with Edith.

Emanating so much power, she understood how he'd once been head of an entire clan and led warriors into battle. His wide shoulders were showcased in the beautifully tailored black Armani jacket. Hair brushed back from his face served only to enhance the man's handsome face and masculine jawline, the color of his eyes brought out by his matching green tie. What surprised Gwen the most was how at ease he moved in the modern clothing, as he crossed the room to greet her.

The picture of him storming into her room this morning

had been totally different. In untucked pullover and slacks, he'd looked more the medieval man, especially with the added element of the angry scowl.

Tightening the towel around her, Gwen walked out of the bathroom and straight into the chest of the man who occupied all her thoughts. Startled, she gasped, jumping back.

"Ye have been avoiding me," Tristan told her, seemingly oblivious to her state of undress. "Why?"

If she ever saw Prince Sterling again, she'd tell him how much his words affected her. *The truth*. Fine. She'd be totally honest, and hope for the best.

"It hurts to see you," she began. "It hurts not to see you. When I am near you, I can't help but think of how much it will hurt when I'm going to be away from you forever. I think that perhaps the more I avoid you, the easier it will be when I leave, only to find it hurts too. I am hoping that by spending time with you, only when others are around, it won't be as bad. Understand me, Tristan, I've never felt as strongly about any man. I have never been in love, before. I'm trying to deal with everything the best I can."

His face softened as he reached and caressed the side of her face. "I am not well trained in the ways of courting a woman. But if ye would allow me, I will tell ye what I think on the matter."

She swallowed the lump that had formed in her throat and nodded.

He looked directly into her eyes, then away, seeming to gather his thoughts. "I can't breathe."

"What?"

"Let me speak, lass. I cannot breathe when I am not near ye. It is the reason I returned early from Edinburgh. I couldn't sleep away from ye. I am satisfied to know ye are under the same roof as I am. When ye are with me, I feel that all will be well. Like ye, I have never felt this way, but I find that I like it." He smiled at her and brushed a tear away as it slipped down her cheek. "I will do anything within my power so that ye never leave me. I love ye, Lady Gwyneth."

Placing his hands on her hips, he brought her to him, his mouth crashing down on hers. Gwen sighed—never had she felt so happy.

He was hers!

Sliding her hands up around his neck, she ran her fingers through his hair as their tongues intermingled.

When he cupped her butt and pulled her closer, his hardness pulsed against her stomach. She stood on her tiptoes to allow for a more intimate closeness.

With a loud moan, he picked her up and carried her to the bed, falling onto it with her. Unfazed that her towel fell away, she quickly unbuttoned his shirt and pushed it off his shoulders while he unfastened his pants. Her intake of breath caught his attention, and he looked down at his black briefs.

"Wow, you look great in those briefs," she told him, her gaze eating up the picture he made, almost nude, his bulging member restrained by the thin fabric.

"They are most uncomfortable, but if ye like them…" He shrugged and moved to her.

"I like them," she told him, nibbling on his bottom lip. The tease worked as he came over her, kissing her neck, teasing her sensitive skin down to her breasts. One hand on one breast, while his tongue did the most delicious things to the other, sent heat coursing through her and she hissed in pleasure.

"Oh, God," Gwen gasped, her hand tight on his shoulders.

"I must have ye now," Tristan told her, his eyes dark emerald with passion.

He pushed his briefs down far enough so that his erection popped free. She reached to caress the velvety soft skin that covered his hardness, guiding him to her. Tristan moaned, throwing his head back.

Sliding into her, the heat of their union brought a scream from her. He moved almost completely out of her before thrusting back in. Gwen met each of his plunges, fighting to keep from losing control. She was not successful. Not even four full thrusts and she totally lost control, falling over the edge, not seeing, not caring, only she and Tristan existing. A few moments later, his loud growl told her he'd joined her.

They made love a second time, this time slowly, taking time to explore each other until not an inch of flesh was left undiscovered. Sated, Gwen lay on Tristan's chest.

A satisfied smile on his face, he lay with one arm under his head, looking up at the ceiling, while she traced circles on his bare chest with her finger.

"You are to remain here in my home; therefore we must marry, of course," he told her, a slight uncertainty in his beautiful green eyes when they met hers.

"I do have a question. Something that has bothered me."

Gwen looked at Tristan. "Derrick said that you were betrothed and killed her."

His eyebrows shot up. "I was never betrothed and certainly have never killed a woman."

Gwen shook her head. "I was certain he'd made it up to turn me away from helping to free you."

"When I see him, I will throttle him."

He'd always be a medieval man, no matter what, and Gwen knew she'd have to accept it.

"No you won't, and yes, I will marry you and stay in Scotland. But promise me, no violence." she replied, kissing him lightly on the lips.

After a moment, Tristan nodded and kissed her soundly.

"I see you two made up," Sabrina told them. "Awesome."

Gwen scrambled, yanking up the sheets to cover her breasts and Tristan's nudity. "Sabrina, you could have knocked—what if you'd walked in on...." She frowned at Tristan, who smiled at Sabrina nonplussed. He was probably used to servants walking in on him nude when he'd been laird.

Sabrina shook her head. "I waited like twenty minutes after Tristan's last growl."

"Sabrina!" Gwen exclaimed, mortified at her sister's words. Tristan patted her shoulder, laughter rumbling in his chest.

"Ye will make Gavin a fine partner," Tristan told Sabrina, whose entire demeanor entirely changed to terror, her eyes wide.

"Partner?"

"Aye. Gavin has the power of seduction. It's part of

breaking his enchantment. He will seduce you into marrying him."

Sabrina squeaked, her eyes flying to Gwen's. "Nope, not happening."

This time it was Gwen's laughter that spilled over. "I can't wait."

Epilogue

For a bunch of extremely wealthy people, the McRainey clan proved to be very down-to-earth. Gwen and Edith's picnic idea for the family reunion was a huge success.

Large tables were scattered on the front lawn, surrounded by family members greeting one another, the women hugging and men shaking hands. The boisterous laughter of children rang out as they scampered about, dodging their mother's attempts to get them to sit down and eat.

Gwen excused herself from a group of women to look for Tristan. She feared he'd be overwhelmed and had perhaps withdrawn into the house.

Walking down the pathway towards the Dunimarle Castle, she hesitated to look up at the large building.

Home. This was to be her new home. They'd agreed to a civil ceremony in town later in the month, with only a few attending, her sisters and mother included. She looked back to the family gathered together enjoying the sunny day, and smiled. It could not be taken for granted. Times like these were rare.

Hearing her future husband's husky laugh, she changed direction toward the side of the house, stopping when she saw him with Derrick.

Tristan placed his hand on Derrick's shoulder. "Of course you are welcome to return. I hoped you would have reconsidered your feelings about me by now. You are family and I look forward to getting to know you better."

Derrick nodded speechless, and then he embraced Tristan.

Gwen went to turn away, but stopped when Tristan called her over. The expression on Derrick's face upon seeing her made her almost feel bad for him, but she merely nodded at him.

"I hope that one day you'll forgive me for my actions."

Gwen met Tristan's eyes briefly before addressing Derrick. "I think I got my pay-back beating the crap out of you with my pillow." She touched his arm. "I'm glad you're here, Derrick."

He nodded, obviously relieved. "Thank you."

"Hey, what are you doing over here?" Sabrina walked up. "The party is over there." She told them pointing towards the front lawn. "Tristan, your Uncle Clive wants you on his croquet team."

Tristan pulled Gwen into his side, kissing her forehead. "Aye, today we will enjoy. After this day, there will be no time for enjoyment; the freedom of the men I left behind will become our focus."

As Derrick and Sabrina headed back to the gathering, Tristan pulled Gwen back. Lifting her face, he kissed her deeply.

"I love you, Gwyneth Lockhart."

She'd never tire of hearing those words. She kissed him back.

Countless challenges still loomed ahead. The others were still trapped, awaiting their rescue. Time was slipping through their fingers. But today—just for today—they allowed themselves to breathe, to feel a fleeting moment of happiness. Tomorrow, the battle would rage once more, with lives hanging in the balance.

Also by Hildie McQueen

The Cursed Kingdom
An Enchanted Knight

Clan Ross
A Heartless Laird

A Hardened Warrior

A Hellish Highlander

A Flawed Scotsman

A Fearless Rebel

A Fierce Archer

Clan Ross of Skye
The Wolf

The Hawk

The Raven

The Falcon

Guards of Clan Ross
Erik

Torac

Struan

Clan Ross of the Hebrides

The Lion

The Beast

The Eagle

The Fox

The Stag

The Duke

The Wildcat

The Hunter

The Bear

Rogues of the Lowlands

A Rogue to Reform

A Rogue to Forget

A Rogue to Cherish

A Rogue to Ensnare

Historical Scottish Novellas

Declan's Bride: A Highland Romp

Ian's Bride: A Highland Rom 2

The Lyon's Laird

Medieval Highlander Romance: The Seer

Pirates of Britannia

The Sea Lion

The Sea Lord

Laurel Creek Series

Jaded: Luke

Brash: Frederick

Broken: Taylor

Ruined: Tobias

Brides for All Seasons

Christina

Sarah

Wilhelmina

Aurora

Lucille

Esther

Scarlet

Isabel

Montana Cowboys

Montana Bachelor

Montana Boss

Montana Beau

Montana Bred

Montana Born

Montana Born & Bred

Shades of Blue

Big Sky Blue

A Different Shade of Blue
The Darkest Blue
Every Blue Moon
Blue Horizon
Montana Blue
Midnight Blue
Shades of Blue Boxed Set
Blue Montana Christmas

Historical Western Romance
Judith, Bride of Wyoming
Patrick's Proposal

Westbound Series
Where the Four Winds Collide
Westbound Awakening

The Fords of Nashville
Even Heroes Cry
The Last Hero
Nobody's Hero

The Moriag series
The Beauty and the Highlander
The Lass and the Laird
Lady and the Scot

The Laird's Daughter

Highland Medieval Romance

Highlander - The Archer

The Duke's Fiery Bride

Contemporary & Western Romance

Melody of Secrets

Taming Lisa

Cowboy in Paradise

About the Author

***USA Today* bestselling author Hildie McQueen** brings action, romance, and unique settings to life in her captivating stories. From sweeping Scottish historical romance to thrilling contemporary romances, her books offer something for every reader to devour!

When she's not weaving tales, Hildie loves diving into a good book, connecting with fans at events, exploring new places, and spending time with her three adorable pups. She lives in the charming small town in Georgia with her superhero husband, Kurt, who makes every day an adventure.